Everyone Needs
A Day Off

There comes a time in every young man's life when
the pressures of school and family routine become
too much. When his instinct to survive overpowers
his ability to reason. When he absolutely must fake
out his parents and his teachers and blow off a day
of school. When he must head downtown with his
best friend and his girl to see the sights, experience
a day of freedom and show that with a little ingenuity,
a lot of courage, and a red Ferrari, life at eighteen
can be a joy.

That's...

Ferris
Bueller's
Day Off

Ferris Bueller's Day Off

A NOVEL
BY TODD STRASSER

BASED ON THE SCREENPLAY
WRITTEN BY JOHN HUGHES

with 8 pages of photos

A SIGNET BOOK

NEW AMERICAN LIBRARY

PUBLISHER'S NOTE
This novel is a work of fiction. Names, characters, places, and
incidents either are the product of the author's imagination or are
used fictitiously, and any resemblance to actual persons, living or
dead, events, or locales is entirely coincidental.

Copyright © 1986 by Paramount Pictures Corporation

SIGNET, SIGNET CLASSIC, MENTOR, PLUME, MERIDIAN
and NAL BOOKS are published by New American Library,
1633 Broadway, New York, New York 10019

First Printing, June, 1986

1 2 3 4 5 6 7 8 9

PRINTED IN THE UNITED STATES OF AMERICA

1

THE suburban village of Shermer, Illinois seems quite unremarkable at first glance. Tree-lined streets are clean, lawns are properly trimmed, and two-story houses are in good repair. It's what people call a bedroom community because just about everyone who lives in Shermer goes off to jobs in Chicago or to school in the morning and returns in the evening to have dinner, sleep, wake up, and repeat the same routine. People here believe that honesty, hard work, and determination breed happiness and prosperity. In short, the American dream still lives in Shermer.

Of course some families have fancier cars than others; some vacation in Europe while others drive to the country for long weekends, but in general the people of Shermer, like their houses, seem very much alike. At least on the outside.

Inside one of those large, colonial houses on a peaceful morning was proof, however, that rarely is anything what it seems.

The Bueller household was alive with early morning activity. Alarms rang, toasters popped, hair dryers hummed. Eighteen-year-old Ferris Bueller—a staunch believer in life, liberty, and the pursuit of happiness—was contemplating the best way to achieve the latter two points on this beautiful spring day. After all, days like this were to be savored. Ferris knew that, he was sure the founding fathers of America had known that—they had just gotten sidetracked with busy work when they instituted things like mandatory school attendance even on warm spring days. It was hard to pursue happiness in high school on days like today, Ferris thought. Like, anybody who says high school is fun isn't in high school or they're from another country. Obviously, politicians were no longer in high school when they thought it would be a great idea for everyone to go to school for eighteen years.

Ferris excused them. Adults often lost sight of simple truths once they got caught up in the bureaucracy of life. Little kids, on the other hand, called the shots as they saw them. Ferris turned on his side in bed and listened to his younger brother and sister down the hall.

"Idiot!"

"Twerp!"

"Nerdball!"

"Scruzball!"

"Listen," Kimberly said, lowering her voice. "When you turn ten your head's going to swell up real big like a watermelon and we're going to have to put you to sleep like they do with a dog."

"You're a liar!" Ricky said.

"I swear to God, it's true," Kimberly replied. "Dr. Albert told me yesterday when I went for my checkup. Mom and Dad have known for years."

Ricky's eyes widened. "Why didn't they tell me?"

"They wanted you to enjoy life for as long as you could," Kimberly said coolly. She couldn't believe he was falling for this one.

"You're lying!" Ricky again insisted, though a tear did crease in the corner of his eye.

"Oh yeah? Looks to me like your head's starting to swell already."

"MOM!" Ricky screamed. He didn't really believe his sister, but it didn't hurt to check things out. A head the size of a watermelon would not be fun. If only Kimberly would move away from the door so he could run down to his parents' room.

"Katie!" Tom Bueller yelled for his wife as he searched through his suit jackets. "Where's my wallet?" He checked the bureau and ruffled through the papers he'd thrown on the night table. No wallet, but at least he'd found his keys. Stuffing them into his pants pocket, he headed for the kitchen. "Katie!"

Just then Ricky skidded past Kimberly and saw his father in the hallway.

"Where's your mother?" Tom asked impatiently.

"Is my head going to swell up?" Ricky looked at his father, half expecting doom.

"What?!" Tom asked as he finished buttoning his shirt. Sometimes he wondered if he heard these kids right. He turned toward the stairs figuring Katie was in the kitchen getting breakfast ready.

"Follow me downstairs, Ricky," Tom added. "I don't know what you're talking about and I have to look for my wallet or I'll be late for work."

"But Kimberly said..." Just then his sister's arms caught him from behind. His father was already gone.

"Wait! Hold still!" she whispered.

"What is it?"

"It is starting to swell up!"

Ricky screamed, but another voice yelled louder. Jeanie Bueller had just finished showering and was reaching for a towel. Her hand came back empty.

"Hey, I need a towel," she shouted. She shivered in the cold air. No doubt Ferris had taken the last clean bathtowel and had forgotten to replace it. Never mind that it was a family rule that anytime someone used a towel he was supposed to replace it with a clean one. Ferris didn't have to follow the rules. Her drippo parents didn't make him follow them.

"Listen," she yelled again, opening the bathroom door just a crack. Water dripped on the floor. "If any of you morons can hear me, I'm freezing to death in the bathroom because some jerk-off took the last bathtowel and didn't replace it."

"Watch your mouth, young lady," her mother shouted back from somewhere in the house.

"Well, are you going to let me freeze to death or what?" Jeanie yelled.

"I'll get to you as soon as I can," Mrs. Bueller replied. "There are other human beings in this family."

Jeanie grumbled and shut the door. There were no other human beings in her family. There was just Ferris the Favorite and four earthworms.

Ferris heard the bathroom door slam. He couldn't understand why Jeanie viewed life as an ordeal that had to be endured. At times it seemed like her body was just a transport vehicle for her anger. Ferris didn't know where she got it from; he certainly enjoyed life, and basically, the rest of the family was pretty cool. In fact, Jeanie was a very attractive seventeen-year-old and he remembered lots of times when they had played together as kids. So why did she get so weirded out every once in a while?

This eccentricity didn't bother Ferris as much as it used to. He had realized that every household has

its little idiosyncracies when he met his best friend
Cameron Frye's family.

Now Cameron's home life was really twisted. Ferris
didn't like going to Cameron's house because it reminded him of a museum. It was very beautiful and
very cold and no one was allowed to touch anything.
In fact, if you opened any door, you'd see that all the
screws in the hinges went straight up and down. Last
year Ferris had turned one of the screws on a hinge
on a kitchen cabinet. He went back to the house a
few days later and the screws had all been turned
back straight up and down again. Ever since that day
Ferris appreciated what it must have been like for
Cameron to grow up in that joint as a baby.

The thought was chilling to Ferris. All his life he'd
lived in a house where each individual left his or her
little mark in various rooms. The atmosphere was
more relaxed, the furniture more comfortable from
wear. Ferris's own bedroom was littered with posters,
magazines, albums of all kinds, a few were strewn
on his night table along with a framed photograph
of his girlfriend, Sloane. Ferris had kept all the model
cars he had assembled as a kid and stuck them on a
shelf next to his catcher's mask and a U.S. army can-
teen. A fluorescent light that flickered *This Bud's for
You* on and off shown from a wall plastered with
posters of Bryan Ferry, The Smiths, and Simple Minds.
Tinier pictures of rock musicians were taped to all
other available wall space, and a British flag hung
from the back of his door.

In fact, all of Ferris's most prized possessions—
from his Carver stereo equipment, Sony CD player,
and Bose speakers to his collection of street signs
and horseshoes—were in this room. It was clearly
his territory, designed and molded by Ferris through-

out the years. There was something very comforting about it, and Ferris couldn't imagine living in anything but the simply organized chaos he added bits and pieces to from time to time. When he played his electric guitar in this room, he felt alive.

Cameron, on the other hand, often felt sick. Ferris was certain his friend's health was seriously impaired by his mausoleumlike surroundings. It was no wonder the poor guy was so uptight. In fact, Cameron was the only guy Ferris knew who felt better when he was sick...

That's it! Ferris knew exactly how he was going to make the most out of this gorgeous day. He was going to pretend he was sick, stay home from school, and call Cameron. No doubt Cam could use fresh air and some fun. It would do him good.

Ferris realized he'd have to act quickly. Any minute now his mother would get Jeanie a towel and then pop her head into his room and ask him what he wanted for breakfast. He had to look deathly ill if he was to convince her—for the ninth time this semester—that he couldn't possibly go in to school today.

Which sickness could he feign this time? Two weeks ago he had done the old hot towel on the forehead fever, and the dog-food-in-the-toilet imitation barf had worked like a charm last semester. The twenty-four-hour whooping cough was always a good one. Naw, that's getting overdone, Ferris thought to himself, and it made his mother too nervous. There was no sense in worrying her over nothing. Besides, if he used that routine today, she'd probably want to take him to the doctor and the only thing worse than school was winding up in Dr. Albert's office.

He'd just lick his palms until they felt clammy and pretend he saw things blurrily. Nonspecific symptoms were always best. Then, if he faked a stomach cramp and doubled over, moaning and wailing, his mother would definitely believe him. Sure, it's a little childish, Ferris realized, but so is high school.

Life moves pretty fast, Ferris thought to himself. If you don't stop once in a while and look around, you could miss it.

Suddenly he heard Ricky running down the hallway to his mother, begging her to tell him whether or not his head was going to swell up and if they would put him to sleep, like the dog. Ferris felt for the kid. You believed that kind of thing when you were seven. Next he heard his mother yelling at Kimberly.

"Leave Ricky alone and go bring a clean towel to Jeanie."

"Do I have to?" Kimberly whined. "She's such a noodge."

"Yes, you have to." Mrs. Bueller replied.

Just then Jeanie's voice sounded through the upper half of the Bueller household. "Who pissed on the toilet seat? MOTHER!"

Kimberly rolled her eyes and, grabbing a towel from the closet nearby, headed for the bathroom. Katie looked at her watch and walked into Ferris's room.

"Ferris, are you up?" She saw him lying in bed. "What's wrong? Why are you still in bed?"

This was it. Instead of answering, he moaned. He knew his mother would have to come closer if she was going to notice his sickly appearance. His mouth opened, tongue hanging out, Ferris groaned again. He sounded like a sick water buffalo. God, could he really pull it off this time, he wondered, wailing more loudly than ever.

But Katie Bueller approached the bed, a worried look on her face. She wore a gray business suit, her hair pulled back to reveal gold earrings in the shape of scallop shells. She touched her palm to Ferris's forehead.

"Ferris, what is it? Please talk to me. What hurts?"

"Thummik," he gasped.

"Thummik?" Katie repeated, not quite understanding.

Ferris slowly lifted his arm and pointed to his stomach.

"Oh, your stomach." Katie finally got it.

Ferris nodded weakly and squinted his eyes, pretending to try to focus on his mother who was looking directly at him.

"Pots," he mumbled.

"Pots?" Joyce echoed.

Ferris gestured to his eyes.

"You're seeing *spots?*" his mother asked. "Oh God, I'd better call a doctor."

"No," Ferris pleaded. "I'll live, really."

But Katie Bueller had seen enough. She hurried to the door and screamed for her husband.

Premenstrual syndrome, Jeanie thought. She bent over the toilet and wiped the little wet droplets off it with tissue paper. Didn't some woman in New Mexico claim that was the reason she murdered her husband? A team of medical experts had gone into court and testified that it was definitely possible that premenstrual syndrome had made the woman crazy enough to kill her husband because he'd forgotten to water her flowers. Well, Jeanie thought, if it was good enough for her, it should be good enough for me. She knew exactly how the toilet seat had gotten wet. Ferris had gotten up in the middle of the night and used the bathroom. Her brother had notoriously bad aim. The jury would understand. Considering the fact that she was suffering from premenstrual syndrome, Jeanie couldn't possibly be found guilty for murdering someone who pissed all over toilet seats.

Ferris lay in bed wondering if there would be enough time to call Sloane before she left for school. His mother was still waiting in the doorway for her husband to arrive. Ferris could hear his father's footsteps racing across the downstairs. His eyeballs were starting to itch and his right arm, the one hanging loosely off the bed, was falling asleep. He waited until his mohter looked away and then quickly licked his hands again. Jeez, he thought, this is hard work.

Ferris heard heavy thuds as his father climbed the stairs two steps at a time. A second later Mr. Bueller appeared in the doorway, wearing a tan business suit, a white shirt, and a bright red tie.

"What's the matter?" he asked his wife, gasping for breath.

"It's Ferris," she said.

Mr. Bueller looked over at the bed. "What's wrong?"

"What's wrong? For Christ's sake! Look at him!"

His parents approached the bed simultaneously, as if together they could combat whatever dread disease had stricken their son.

"Ferris?" his father said, kneeling next to the bed. Ferris didn't answer. He knew from experience that it was better to let his parents' imaginations run wild.

"He doesn't have a fever," Katie Bueller said, "but he says his stomach hurts and he's seeing spots."

Tom Bueller touched his son's forehead. "What's the matter, Ferris?"

Ferris just moaned.

"Feel his hands. They're cold and clammy," Katie said.

Mr. Bueller touched one of Ferris's hands. "And a

little slimy," he said. "Should you call the doctor?"

"He doesn't want me to," Katie said.

"Why don't you want Mom to call the doctor?" his father asked.

Ferris moved his lips as if he were struggling to get the words out. "Dooooooon't. Don't make a fuss. I'm fine," he said hoarsely. "I'll get up." He started to sit up but his mother reached forward and touched his shoulder. Ferris allowed her to push him back down. That was always a good sign. Now he just had to throw in the final touch.

"I have a test today," he said, making his voice raspy. "I have to take it. I want to get into a good college so I can have a successful life..."

"You're not going to school like this," Mrs. Bueller insisted.

Ferris knew he had it made, but he couldn't resist one last scene. "I'm okay, Mom. I feel perfectly—" Suddenly he was gripped by a seizure. "Oh, God!"

Jeanie Bueller applied her makeup in the bathroom. She brushed her blond hair and checked her clothes in the mirror. Hearing the commotion down the hall, she knew it concerned Ferris. All commotions in the family concerned Ferris. If something happened to her, on the other hand, no one would raise an eyebrow. Her brother got all the attention, while she got none. That was the way it had always been, and was probably the way it would always be.

Jeanie decided to see what the noise was about this time. As she walked down the hall toward Ferris's room, she imagined herself in the courtroom before the judge: *I'm sorry, your honor, I realize now that it was wrong to strangle my brother with panty hose, but at the time I was suffering from premenstrual syndrome and I knew he had peed on the toilet seat.*

Thank you for letting me go free. I promise to be good for the rest of my life.

She got to Ferris's room and saw him lying in bed, looking like he'd just swallowed a lab experiment. God, if only it was true, she thought. Her parents were hovering over the bed, playing "General Hospital."

"Oh, fine. What's this? What's *his* problem?" Jeanie asked, her hands on her hips, her foot tapping on the floor.

"He doesn't feel well," her mother said, without turning around.

Jeanie smiled and moved toward her brother's desk. She casually picked up one of his model submarines. "Yeah, right. Dry that one out and you can fertilize the lawn."

Her father gave her a sharp look. "That's enough, Jeanie."

"You're not falling for this, are you?" Jeanie asked. "Tell me you're not falling for this."

In the bed, Ferris stirred. "Is that Jeanie? I can't see that far. Jeanie?"

"Pucker up and squat, Ferris."

"Thank you, Jeanie," her mother said testily. "Now get to school."

But Jeanie didn't budge. "You're really letting him stay home?" she asked. "I can't believe this. If I was bleeding out my eyes, you guys would make me go to school. It's so unfair."

Ferris stirred again. "Please don't be upset with me, Jeanie. Be thankful that you're fit and have your health. Cherish it."

"Oh, I want to puke!" Jeanie shouted. She slammed the model down, turned, and stormed to the stairs. It was so incredibly unfair. How could they believe every lie her brother told them? How did he get away with it? She couldn't figure it out; all she knew was that he infuriated her. Such an incredible liar! Such a brat! And yet everyone loved him. She just couldn't understand it.

Ferris listened to the thumping of Jeanie descending the stairs. He couldn't understand why she took this stuff so seriously. If anything, she could have gotten the hint and played sick herself. It was perfectly logical that she could have caught it from him. Then at least, he'd definitely have someone to hang out with all day. Meanwhile, both of his parents were checking their watches. Thank God he lived in a two-income family and his parents had nine-to-five jobs to get to.

Kimberly and Ricky stuck their faces in the doorway. Kimberly, at twelve, was still dressing like a Madonna clone because no one new had come along for her to immitate. Ricky, even deeper in the ozone, still let their mother pick his clothes.

"Myocardial infarction?" Kimberly whispered.

Mr. Bueller turned toward her and shook his head.

"Stroke?" Kimberly asked.

"Get your stuff," her mother said. "Daddy'll be right down."

"Syphilitic meningitis?" Kimberly said. "That would be a huge family embarrassment."

Ferris had a hard time keeping a straight face. His sister would make a great comedienne someday.

"Go!" Mr. Bueller yelled. "Mom'll be down in a minute."

Kimberly backed toward the door. "Okay, but if he dies, I got dibs on his stereo." She took off, leaving Ricky in the doorway.

"And what do you want?" his mother asked.

Ricky pointed to his skull. "Does my head still look all right?"

"Get downstairs," Mrs. Bueller said.

"God, if it was your head," Ricky whined. He really was concerned and no one seemed to care.

"Now!" Tom Bueller shouted.

Ferris watched his brother dash from the doorway. Three gone, two to go. He took a deep breath and let it out slowly. He was almost there. "Mom? Dad? I think I'll be okay. I'll just sleep. Maybe I'll have an aspirin around noon."

Mrs. Bueller nodded. "I have to show a house to that family from Los Angeles today. I know they're just inches from making a decision. If you need me and I'm not in the office, someone there will know where to reach me."

"And I'll be in my office all day," his father said. "If you need anything, anything at all, just call me, okay?"

Ferris nodded weakly. "It's nice to know I have such loving, caring parents. You're both very special people."

His mother reached forward and stroked his hair. "And we think you are very special too."

His father put his hand gently on his shoulder. "Remember, if you need anything...Okay, pal?"

Ferris nodded slowly, as if it took all the strength he had. Then he closed his eyes as if he was too weak to keep them open any longer.

His mother bent forward and kissed him on the forehead. "Feel better, pumpkin."

"I will, Mom," he said, in a voice just above a whisper.

His parents got up and moved quietly toward the door, as if they were afraid to disturb him.

"We love you, sweetie," his mother whispered.

"Don't forget the phone," his father said in a low voice.

Ferris remained motionless ad looking close to death. Finally he heard the door close and the lock click. He opened one eye just a sliver and looked around to make sure. His room was empty. He opened both eyes and rolled onto his back, resting his right arm back on the bed to let the blood flow back into it. They bought it, he thought. Unbelievable. One of the worst performances of his career and they never doubted it for a second. He sat up and stretched his arms out wide. It had to be the clammy hands that convinced them. Nothing like a good, nonspecific symptom.

2

A ROCK video played on the TV monitor but Ferris couldn't hear the song. The sound was turned off while he called Sloane's house. Mrs. Petersen answered. "Hello?"

"Hey, Mrs. P.," Ferris said. "Did Sloane split for school yet?"

"Yes, she did, Ferris," Mrs. Petersen replied, her voice cool and distant. It was a tone he was used to. It said that she thought he was nothing better than white middle-class suburban trash.

"Well, thanks anyway, Mrs. P. And by the way, have your crocus come up yet?"

She hung up on him. Ferris put the phone back on the hook and shook his head. Why were parents so weird? He knew she was into stuff like crocuses and he was only trying to be polite. So how come when he asked about them, she hung up on him? He could never understand why all his friends' parents hated him. After all, his own parents adored him.

Well, there was no point in worrying about it. He jumped out of bed and turned up the volume on the stereo. The song blasted from the speakers as he yanked open the drapes. Modern meteorological technology was wonderful, he thought. Just as promised on the news the night before, the sky was blue—

19

not a cloud in sight. How could anyone possibly expect him to handle school on a day like this?

Ferris stayed by the window and watched the family armada roll out of the three-car garage. Jeanie's new white Fiero was the first out the gate, followed by his father's maroon Audi, and his mother in the station wagon.

Ferris watched as the station wagon turned around the corner and disappeared. He still couldn't believe his parents had bought this morning's act. It had been worse than sub-dinner theater. If they could fall for that, the possibilities of what else they'd go for were frightening. If they were Eskimos, he could probably sell them snow. Too bad he had some conscience.

Ferris crouched down in front of his stereo and turned up the bass. The room filled with booming music. He fiddled with the dials, equalized the levels a little. Nine for nine, he thought. If I ever decide to go for ten, I'll probably have to barf up a lung. Better make today count—it could be the last day off for a while.

He swung out into the hall and headed for the bathroom. Jeez, what a pigsty! Jeanie's junk was everywhere. Blow dryers, trays full of makeup, pimple cream, brushes, combs, cans of shaving cream, styling mousse, little wads of crumpled tissue, used Q-tips. Ferris picked up an eyelash curler and scowled at it. Was this really necessary? How could she complain about anything when all this stuff was hers?

Looking in the mirror, he wondered why people really bothered with makeup. His brown hair and dark eyes seemed all right to him and changing colors wouldn't ever make him different from what he was ... so why bother?

He reached into the shower and turned it on, holding his hand under the spray until the temperature was just right. Then he climbed in and began to compose that morning's lecture. It was a routine he observed every morning—it got his creative juices going. The title this morning was:

Cut and Don't Get Caught: The Fine Points of Ditching by Ferris Bueller.

As he soaped up in the shower he imagined himself standing at a podium before a huge crowd of kids: *I'd like to thank you all for cutting school and coming to hear me today. As you know, the topic of my talk will be ditching. You might be interested to know that I have just come from Harvard, where I gave an intensive three-month seminar on the subject that was so effective no one showed up on the last day.*

Many of you probably think it's a waste of time to come to a lecture about ditching, right? You're probably asking yourself, What's the big deal? If you want to ditch, you just ditch, right?

Wrong. Ditching is a complicated activity. It must be approached in an organized way, especially if you plan to make a career of it.

For instance, one very serious danger in playing sick is that if you do it often enough and well enough, it's possible to believe your own act. I know people who get so psyched up for their act that it takes them most of the day just to feel well again!

And then there's the boredom factor. Many people ditch and feel great for about an hour. Then they realize that they have nothing to do but eat and watch TV. I myself have ditched and gotten so bored that I did homework!

So the most important preparation you can do for a day of ditching is make a plan. Otherwise you're just gonna sit around worrying about what to do.

And what do you need that grief for? Especially when the whole point is to take it easy, cut loose, and enjoy it.

That concludes my lecture for today. Go out and have a good time, but don't forget to bring a note from your parents to school tomorrow. Remember, the day after you graduate you will forget everything you ever learned in high school, but forgery is a skill that lasts a lifetime. Thank you.

Twenty minutes later he headed downstairs, dressed in a T-shirt and sweat pants. It was one of his better lectures, he thought as he walked into the kitchen and took a bag of Oreos out of the pantry. Too bad the world wasn't ready for it. He reached for the wall phone and started to dial.

3

OCCASIONALLY, someone in high school actually became legitimately ill and had to stay home for a day. In a sleek, modern, glass and steel house almost hidden in woods several miles from Ferris's house, Cameron Frye lay in bed listening to a new rock cassette and staring at the ceiling. Cameron had dark hair and eyes, was slightly on the stocky side, but all in all considered rather lovable looking. Except when his face was as pale as it was right now.

Next to his bed was a table filled with every kind of cold medicine, nasal spray, and throat lozenge imaginable. All the bottles and tubes were arranged on a white lacquer tray. Medical gadgets from heating pads to a home blood-pressure unit were positioned neatly in the room within Cameron's reach. A humidifier hummed softly from the corner, spraying the room with a fine mist that balanced the air's moisture. The bedroom was dimly lit; the curtains remained closed.

The phone rang. Cameron removed the electronic thermometer from his mouth and pressed the speaker phone button. "Hello," he said, his voice devoid of energy.

"Hey, Cam, what's happening?" Ferris's cheerful voice filled the deathly still room.

"Very little," Cameron replied. He should have known it would be Ferris.

"How do you feel?" Ferris asked as a matter of course.

"Shredded," he responded, making sure the armband to the blood-pressure unit was properly secured so he'd get a good reading.

"Your mother in the room?" Ferris asked.

"She's in Decatur. Unfortunately, she's not staying. Where are you?"

"I'm taking the day off. Get dressed and come over."

"I can't. I'm sick," Cameron said firmly.

"It's all in your head. Come on over." Ferris was used to hearing Cameron's complaints. Rarely did he believe any of them.

"I feel like complete shit, Ferris. I can't go anywhere."

That meant he should go everywhere, Ferris thought. "I'm sorry to hear that. Now come on over and pick me up." He hung up the phone.

Cameron switched off the speaker box and checked the reading on the blood-pressure unit. "I'm dying," he moaned, just as the phone rang again. He hit the button.

"You're not dying. You just can't think of anything to do." Ferris's voice reverberated in the room before he hung up.

Ferris sat on the couch in the family room for a minute after he finished talking to Cameron. If anybody needs a day off, it's Cameron, he thought. He has a lot of things to sort out before he graduates. He can't be wound this tight and go to college; his roommate will kill him. I've come close myself a few times.

But I like him. He's a little easier to take when you know why he's like he is. The boy cannot relax. There's always a fire burning in his head. In fact, Ferris thought, Cameron is so tight that if you stuck a lump of coal up his ass, you'd have a diamond in two weeks. And then Cameron would worry that he'd owe taxes on it.

The guy definitely had to lighten up, Ferris said to himself as he walked back upstairs to Jeanie's room. Strewn with clothes, jewelry, and magazines, his sister's room was a pastel pigsty. Ferris picked up a pink sweat shirt off the floor and tossed it onto a chair. He sat down on his sister's bed and started leafing through *Seventeen* when he noticed a beaded purse on top of an oversize sweater. Regardless of how much grief sisters give you, Ferris thought, you should never alienate one. More often than not they have cash and it's usually very easy to get your hands on. He pulled a twenty-dollar bill from the purse and snapped it in the air while he headed for the living room.

Usually there were coins stuck between the cushions of the couch and today was no exception. He found several sticky quarters in the crevices and even a dollar bill. One of his father's suit jackets was draped across a chair and Ferris extracted five dollars from its pocket. They'll probably never miss this, Ferris thought as he climbed back up to his room. And I'll certainly need it to make my day off worthwhile.

Shermer High School was built in 1955, a year when almost every new suburban high school east of the Rocky Mountains was built in a square shape with a big quadrangle in the middle. At one end of the square was the gymnasium and at the other end was the cafeteria and administrative offices. Stuck somewhere in between was the library and a big science lab. The schools were usually made of red brick and were one story high, except for the gym and cafeteria.

Whoever came up with the design for all these high schools probably envisioned the big grassy quadrangle in the middle of the school as a place where students would gather at lunchtime. The quadrangle also had cement paths so that students could cut across it to get to their classes without having to fight the human traffic in the halls. What the designer didn't realize was that if you sat with your friends in the quadrangle, you would be watched from every side by bored students in classrooms.

That meant that if you picked your nose, a hundred students would see it. If you had a baloney sandwich and you bit into it and a slice of baloney slipped out the other end, there were witnesses. No matter what you did in the quadrangle, it would be seen. Being in the quadrangle was something like being in a cage at the zoo.

So nobody at any of these schools used the quadrangle. They wouldn't even walk across them to get to another class. It was sort of an unwritten code. Only nerds and toads and people who were so out of it they thought Madonna was the Virgin Mary ever went into the quad.

Every day, Jeanie Bueller walked across the quad. She'd been doing it since ninth grade. She had never been able to figure out why no one else, except a few of her friends, used it. It seemed like a much easier way to get to class than pushing your way through all the dorks in the hallway.

In room 109 in Shermer High old Mr. Clark sat down at his desk and placed his black attendance book before him. Mr. Clark taught English and while he couldn't have been past sixty, he looked like teaching at Shermer had aged him well beyond his years. His hair was white and his body was thin, stiff, and bony. He gave you the impression that he didn't care what happened each day in school as long as he survived it.

From his desk drawer, he took out one blue and one red pencil. Then he opened the attendance book and began to read names. "Albers?"

"Here," a kid said.

Mr. Clark made a mark in the book with the blue pencil.

"Baker?"

"Here."

"Baxter?"

"Here."

"Bueller?"

There was no answer.

"Bueller?" Mr. Clark said again.

"He's sick," said a girl in the last row. "My best friend's sister's boyfriend's brother's girlfriend heard from this guy who knows this kid who's going with a girl who saw Ferris pass out at Thirty-one Flavors last night. I guess it's pretty serious."

Mr. Clark nodded wearily and made a mark in his attendance book with the red pencil. "Thank you, Simone."

"No problem whatsoever," Simone said.

Mr. Clark nodded and went back to attendance. "Cleary?"

"Here."

"Corbin?"

"Here."

"Dean?"

"Here."

"Drucker?"

"Here."

"Franklin?"

"Here."

"Frye?"

There was no answer.

"Frye?" Mr. Clark said again.

"I think he joined the Marines," Drucker said. "I saw him in the enlistment office over at the mall after school yesterday."

Mr. Clark looked up in disbelief. "Cameron Frye, a Marine?"

"Well, you know how the Marines are looking for a few good men," Drucker said.

"God help them if they think that means Frye," Mr. Clark said.

The bell rang and homeroom ended. In a classroom down the hall from Mr. Clark's, Sloane Petersen picked up her books and tried to prepare herself for another unexciting day of classes, socializing, and cheerleading practice. Sloane was a junior, about five-eight, brunette, and in the last six months she had suddenly blossomed into the best-looking girl in school. She was also one of the most popular girls in school, as well as one of the best cheerleaders. Not only that, but her grade average was 3.77.

Based on those statistics, Sloane Petersen seemed qualified to be just another shallow girlfriend of the captain of the football team. And for a while it almost seemed that she was destined to become one. But someone had intervened and saved her. Someone named Ferris Bueller.

Her friends were kind of surprised when Sloane started seeing Ferris. It was an established fact that everyone liked him, and sure, he was good-looking, but there had to be at least half a dozen guys at school who looked better. He also had a nice build, but Rambo he wasn't. He was a good athlete who didn't take sports seriously, an intelligent guy who didn't particularly care about grades. But there were two things that made Ferris different from all the other guys she'd dated. The first was that he was always fun. Even when he was serious he was fun. And the second thing was that he seemed to know what life was all about. While all the other guys she'd dated were still trying to figure it out, Ferris was way ahead of them. He already knew.

Sloane stepped into the hall. During the day her path rarely crossed Ferris's, but the one time she was always sure to see him was at his locker right after homeroom. Only today he wasn't there. Just at that moment, Jeanie Bueller passed by.

"Hey, Jeanie," Sloane said. Ferris's sister gave her a cold look. Sloane couldn't figure out why Jeanie hated her, but then the look on Jeanie Bueller said she hated everyone.

"Isn't Ferris here today?" Sloane asked.

"He's ditching," Jeanie said, and walked away.

Ditching? Sloane thought. Why didn't he take me with him? She turned and headed toward class. For the first time since she'd met Ferris, she was disappointed in him.

4

FERRIS had wanted a car for Christmas, but he'd gotten a computer instead. At first he'd been disappointed, but then he'd decided that beggars couldn't be choosy. True, you couldn't drive around in a computer, but it had to be good for something. He'd gotten Cameron to come over and explore the possibilities. Among Cameron's numerous talents was an uncanny understanding of how electronic devices such as phone-answering machines, intercoms, doorbells, and tape recorders could be made to work in harmony through an Apple IIe.

Over the course of three afternoons during Christmas vacation, he and Cameron had wired almost every electronic device in the house to the computer. His parents didn't know it, but if Ferris wanted to, he could turn on the lights, switch channels on the television, and even run the dishwasher from the console of the computer. But today he didn't have to do any of those things. All he had to do was leave a couple of messages on his tape recorder and telephone-answering machine in case anyone should call. And after covering an old mannequin Ferris had in his room with blankets so it looked like someone was lying in bed, Ferris rigged a wire from the bedroom door handle through a pulley and connected it to the synthesizer. If anyone opened the door, the keyboard would emit a fuzzy tone that sounded remarkably like a snore, which, of course, they would assume was coming from the body buried beneath the covers.

Just then the phone started to ring. Ferris glanced up at the clock. Then he picked up the phone and gave a weak, "Huh—hell—o?"

"Ferris?" his father said.

"D—Dad?" Ferris gasped.

"Are you okay?" Mr. Bueller asked. "You sound terrible."

"No, uh, I'll make it, Dad."

"Did you get some sleep?"

"Well, actually, I've been trying to do some homework, Dad. I'm so worried about college. I can't afford to fall behind."

"Now listen to me, Ferris," Mr. Bueller said, going into his stern fatherly mode. "There's a time for everything and right now it's time for you to rest. You can do the homework when you're better."

"But college, Dad," Ferris said with a nice little gasp for effect.

"Damn it, Ferris, if they don't understand that a boy can't work when he's ill, I'll call them myself and make sure they do."

"Wow, Dad, you're super," Ferris said.

"It's nothing, son. I know how much pressure you're under. But you have a lifetime of pressure ahead of you and there's no sense in overburdening yourself now."

Ferris couldn't help smiling. The power a sick kid had over his parents was amazing. It was the ultimate guilt trip. They didn't want you to know it, but deep down parents blamed themselves for everything that went wrong with their kids. If only he'd come down with something serious before Christmas, he would have gotten a car instead of a computer. It was too late for that, but right now he needed more cash.

"You know, Dad," he said. "It's really great that you called. I bet there're a lot of fathers who wouldn't take time out from their busy work schedules just to call a dumb, sick teenager."

He could almost see his father smiling proudly on the other end of the line. It was easy to make his father happy, and if it made Ferris happy too, there was no harm in a little deception.

"Hey, pal, what was I supposed to do?"

"You really should give yourself credit, Dad. It's a great gesture. Like those savings bonds you used to buy every Christmas for my education. It's that kind of concern."

"Well, like I said, son, what's a father for? I mean, if he can't provide for his kids' future education needs, what good is he?"

Ferris paused to take a sip of Pepsi and then went for it. "You're right, Dad. Come to think of it, whatever happened to those bonds?"

"I've still got them."

"In some bank vault, huh?"

"Nope, right in our house," Mr. Bueller said.

Ferris felt his jaw drop. "No, you're pulling my leg, Pop."

"The hell I am," his father said. "They're in a shoe box in my closet."

"I can't believe it," Ferris said. "I mean, isn't it dangerous to leave them around like that?"

"Listen, son, if you were a burglar rifling through a closet, do you think you'd stop to look in some old smelly shoe box?"

Damn straight I would, Ferris thought.

"Besides," Mr. Bueller went on. "Even if you did, you probably wouldn't see them. They're tucked up inside my old brown wing tips."

So that's why I could never find them, Ferris thought.

"Now listen, son," his father said. "No more schoolwork today. I want you to get some rest."

"I promise, Dad, I'm going right back upstairs as soon as I get off the phone," Ferris said.

"Good. And feel better." Mr. Bueller hung up.

Ferris put the receiver back on the hook and did a little dance on the kitchen floor. Then he turned and went up the stairs and into his parents' room. It only took a second to find the shoe box containing the old wing tips. He opened it and took out the bonds, spreading them out in his fingers like a big hand of playing cards. He looked up at the ceiling. Dear God, he prayed, I know my father worked hard to earn the money for these bonds and that's why, out of all ten, I'm only going to take one. Because, with the exception of this semester, I promise to ditch only one-tenth of the time for as long as my education shall last.

He put the rest of the bonds back in the shoe and stood up. And by the way God, if I ever have kids, please don't let them pull this kind of crap on me. On the other hand, if they didn't pull this kind of crap, they'd be dumb and abnormal and they'd probably never move out of my house and I'd have to support them until I die. He looked up again. Forget what I just said. I take it back.

5

ED Rooney considered himself a reasonable man. As principal of Shermer High, he was neither a kick-butt military drill sergeant nor a limp-wristed peace-and-love wimp. He commanded a clean, efficient ship, but at the same time he wasn't opposed to his crew cutting up once in a while and having a little fun.

There was, however, a limit.

And he had a feeling Ferris Bueller had just overstepped it.

Sitting in his office with his feet up on his desk, Rooney stared at his computer monitor. On the screen, Bueller's name, address, and vital statistics were spelled out. Next to the word "absences," the numeral nine flashed on and off.

And it's only April, Rooney thought.

He knew Bueller was not a sickly boy. If anything, Bueller was healthier than most. And more charming, and more likable. Too goddamned likable, if you ask me, the principal thought.

Rooney swung his feet off his desk, stood up, and straightened his suit. He was a fair-haired, tall, well-built man who took pride in his appearance. Every morning he rowed five miles on his rowing machine while watching the morning news. By his calculations, he'd probably already rowed the equivalent of around the world twice in his life. He did forty push-ups and a hundred sit-ups too. He knew the meaning of hard work and discipline. He knew he had what it took to be elected Outstanding High School Principal of the Year someday.

Ed Rooney stood next to his desk and looked at the computer screen again. During his fifteen years as high school principal he'd known a few kids like Bueller before. They were the cocky kind of kids who thought they could always get by on finesse and good looks. They tried to charm teachers into giving them better grades than they deserved, they tried to sweet-talk their way out of any trouble they got into. They usually had their parents completely hoodwinked. One thing was for certain—they never had to work hard the way Ed Rooney had. They never took jobs after school or shoveled snow on weekends. They never stayed up late at night sweating over their homework. Life came too easily to them, unless they had an Ed Rooney in their lives to straighten them out.

Rooney reached across his desk and pushed down the intercom button on his phone.

Ms. Vine, his secretary answered. "Yes, Mr. Rooney?"

"Ms. Vine, are you familiar with a student here named Ferris Bueller?" Rooney asked.

"Oh, yes, Mr. Rooney," Ms. Vine said. "Why just last week he brought me a beautiful bouquet of flowers. Of course, the card said 'To Dearest Joyce' and my name is Grace, but it was probably just a mistake by the florist."

Rooney chuckled. "I'll bet." He walked to the end

of his office and stood by the window, looking out at the wide lawn and Stonevale Street beyond it. The trees and shrubs were starting to turn green, a couple of convertibles rode past with their tops down. Spring had arrived and with it ditching season. And somewhere out there in the distance, Ferris Bueller thought he was pulling a fast one. The principal smiled. I'm sorry, son, but it's never too late to even the score. He walked back to his desk and pressed the intercom button again.

"Yes, Mr. Rooney?"

"Ms. Vine, please get Ferris Bueller's mother on the line. I want to talk to her."

Time to spread a few harmless rumors, Ferris thought as he picked up the phone and dialed the number of the pay phone near the school office. This was by far his best and most intricate plan ever. It had more phases than the moon. He knew it'd work.

"Yeah?" a kid answered. Sounded like a freshman.

"Hey," Ferris said faintly, "this is Ferris Bueller and I just wanted to say good-bye."

"Oh, I know you, man," the kid said. "Where're you going?"

"I'm going to die," Ferris said.

"No, shit, what's it feel like?"

Ferris scowled. "Well, it feels like they just sent a quart of my blood to Atlanta to the Center for Disease Control. I don't know, man, I'm bricking heavily."

"Wow, you do sound wasted, man," the kid said.

"Yeah. Did you see *Alien*?" Ferris asked. "When that guy had the baby alien in his stomach? It feels like that too."

"Oh, wow," the freshman said.

"So I was wondering if you'd do me a favor and send my regards to everyone, okay?" Ferris said.

"Sure thing, man," the kid said. "Hey, hold on a second."

Ferris could hear the kid yell to someone else in the hall. "Hey, Joey, Ferris Bueller is on the phone. You gotta talk to him, he's bricking heavily." The kid got back on the phone. "Ferris, I gotta split to class, man. Stay cool. Here's Joey."

Joey got on the phone. Ferris didn't know who Joey was, but that didn't matter.

"Hey, man," Joey said. "I hear you're bricking heavily."

"Yeah," Ferris said.

"I know this'll sound dumb," Joey said. "But I never heard of anyone bricking before. Like does it hurt?"

"Did you see *Alien?*" Ferris asked.

"Oh, wow," Joey said. "You mean it's like that?"

"Yeah," Ferris said. "It's really hard on the kidneys."

"I believe it," Joey said.

It sounded like there were voices in the hall behind Joey arguing. Then Joey said he had to get off and a girl got on. "Hi. It's Wanda. How's your bod?"

Ferris repeated his routine once more.

"Oh, my God! You're dying? Is it serious?"

Ferris held the phone away from his ear and stared at it in disbelief. Could she be serious?

"Are you upset?" she asked.

Ferris rolled his eyes. Freshmen were another species altogether.

0806 on Rooney's phone started to flash.

"I've got Mrs. Bueller on the line," Ms. Vine said over the office intercom."

Rooney pushed down the button on the phone. "Hello, Mrs. Bueller?"

"Yes?" a woman's voice answered.

Rooney pressed the phone against his ear. "Mrs. Bueller, this is Principal Rooney over at Shermer High. Are you aware that your son is not in school today?"

"Oh, God, I'm so sorry," Katie Bueller said. "I completely forgot to call. Ferris is home sick. I meant to call but I had a meeting first thing this morning and it completely slipped my mind."

Rooney glanced over at the computer monitor. "Are you also aware that Ferris does not have what we consider an exemplary attendance record?"

"I don't understand," Katie said.

"He's missed an unacceptable number of school days," Rooney said. The number nine still flashed on the screen. "Regardless of what you may think, in the opinion of this educator, Ferris isn't taking his academic growth seriously. Now I've spent my morning examining his records, and if Ferris thinks he can coast these last months and still graduate, he's sorely mistaken. I have no reservations whatsoever about holding him back another year."

"This is all news to me," Katie said.

"It usually is," replied the principal. "Did you know, for instance, that this semester alone he's been absent nine times?"

"Nine times?" Katie found that hard to believe.

"Nine times," Rooney repeated.

"I don't remember him being sick nine times," Katie said.

Rooney smiled. "That's probably because he wasn't sick. He was skipping school. Wake up and smell the coffee, Mrs. Bueller. It's a fool's paradise. He's leading you down the primrose path. I am looking at his attendance record at this very moment, and I—" Rooney stopped in midsentence. Suddenly the number nine flashed to an eight. Then seven, then all the way down to two before holding steady. He sat up straight in his chair, barely hearing Katie Bueller on the other end of the phone.

"I can give you every assurance Mr.—uh." For a second Katie couldn't remember his name. "Rooney, that Ferris is home and that he is very ill. In fact, I debated whether or not I should even leave him. I can appreciate that at this time of year children are prone to taking the day off, but in Ferris's case, I can assure you, he's truly a very sick boy. Now I'd like to stay on and chat, but there are some clients here and I have to take them to see a house. Good-bye, Mr. Rooney." She hung up.

Rooney continued staring at the computer screen. Someone was tapping into the school's computer system. And he had a sneaking suspicion he knew just who that someone was. He hit the side of the computer.

6

FERRIS stared at the Apple computer. His school records were on the screen. He liked the idea of two absences better than nine.

He picked up the phone and dialed Cameron's number. He knew his friend was probably debating with himself as he dressed. He'd have to give him a gentle push.

The phone rang in Cameron's house. The guy won't give up, Cameron thought. He knows I'm here sitting on this bed. He'll hang on all day until I answer. Cameron started to reach for the phone but then stopped. If I answer he'll make me do something I don't want to do. I don't know what it will be, but it will definitely be something I know I'll regret.

The ringing continued. It was starting to give Cameron an even worse headache than he already had. On the other hand, he thought, I already regret having to lie here and listen to this stupid phone ring.

He answered it. "I know it's you, Ferris. I'm sick, I feel like crap. Why can't you leave me alone?"

"Because I care about you," Ferris said. "You're my best friend."

"If you cared about me, you'd leave me alone." Cameron sniffed.

"And let you feel lousy all day?" Ferris asked. "What kind of friend would do a thing like that?"

Cameron blew his nose in some tissues. "Listen, Ferris," he said. "I'm going to feel lousy all day no matter what I do."

"If that's the case, why lie around feeling lousy all by yourself when you could come over here and feel lousy with me?"

"Because at least if I stay here I won't get in trouble," Cameron said. "If I come see you I will not only feel lousy, I'll get in trouble too."

"When have I ever gotten you in trouble?"

Cameron coughed. "Are you serious? The question is, when haven't you gotten me in trouble? You got me to help you paint the water tower, and who got caught? Me. You got me to order a pizza for homeroom, and who got in trouble? Me. Whatever we do, it's always your idea, and I always get caught."

"But you have fun, right?"

"Maybe I have fun while I'm doing it, but the second I get caught it's no longer fun. Then it's just regret."

"Okay, I'll make a promise to you," Ferris said. "I promise you I won't make you do anything today. Just come over and hang out with me. I'm lonely, I need company. You know how it is."

Cameron sighed. "Ferris, you're my best friend, but I don't believe you."

"I swear," Ferris said. "I swear on my entire collection of Talking Heads albums."

"I still don't believe you," Cameron said.

"How can you know for sure unless you come over here and see?" Ferris asked. "Are you willing to go through the rest of your life wondering whether or not I would have kept my promise today? Do you really think you could live with that kind of burden?"

Cameron smiled. "You're so full of it, Ferris."

"I bet you just smiled," Ferris said.

"Did not." Cameron forced the grin off his face.

"Yes, you did. I know you did. I know you, Cameron. And if you'd just come over, we could have a great time today and the only thing that would happen would be that you'd feel better."

Cameron shook his head slowly. He knew it was hopeless. Ferris wouldn't let up until he won. "Someday you're going to be president," he said.

"I know," Ferris said, and hung up.

Twenty minutes later Cameron trudged out to his car, a beat-up Honda Civic. His pockets were stuffed with tissues and pills. He'd just taken two aspirin, a Contact, 2000 mgs of vitamin C, and a snort of Dadril nasal decongestant mist. He got in the Civic, started the engine, and began to back it down the driveway.

Halfway down he stopped. Am I insane? he asked himself. Am I crazy? I've just taken so much junk I'll probably get stopped by a cop and arrested for driving under the influence of cold medications. You see, Cameron? This is what Ferris does to you. You haven't even left your property *and you're already in trouble!*

Cameron shifted the Civic into forward and drove back up the driveway. He parked and got out. I am not having anything to do with him today, he told himself. I am going to be ill all by myself. I may have to suffer alone, but I will do so with the knowledge that I was strong enough to stand up for myself and say no to Ferris.

As soon as he stepped inside the house, the phone started to ring.

Cameron stopped and stared at it. I don't believe this, he thought.

The phone continued to ring.

How does he know?

Ring, ring, ring!

Cameron lunged forward and grabbed the phone. "Listen, douche bag, I've had it. Do you hear? I don't care if you're my best friend, you can't make me do it."

"Do what?" a voice asked.

"Huh?" Cameron said.

"I said, do what?" the voice asked again.

"Oh, shit," Cameron said.

"You're right," the voice said. "No one can make you do that except yourself."

"Uh, look," Cameron said, "I don't know who you are, but I apologize. I've just take a whole lot of cold medications and I'm not right in the head."

"Oh, you don't have to apologize," the voice said.

"Well, who is this?" Cameron asked.

"My name is William McBryson and I'm with Strauss Surveys Incorporated and today we're calling about aerosol deodorants. Have you got five minutes to answer some questions?"

"I'm sorry, Mr. McBryson, but I don't know doodlely squat about aerosol deodorants," Cameron said.

"Oh, well, in that case, thanks for your time." McBryson hung up.

Cameron stared at the phone for a second and then put it down. It immediately started to ring again. He picked it up. "Hello?"

"I know exactly what you just did," Ferris said.

"You do?"

"Yes. You got into your car and backed halfway down the drive way and stopped and decided not to come over."

"Do you have spies or something?" Cameron asked.

"No, but I told you I know you," Ferris said. "And I know that that is exactly what you'd do."

Cameron pressed his fingers against his temples to try to ease the throbbing. He felt weary. "Ferris, I can't."

"You can," Ferris replied. "And what's more, you must."

"Why?"

"Because if anyone needs a day off, it's you," Ferris said. "You don't know this, but I'm concerned about you. You've got a fantastic future, but you're so wound up you'll never make it through college."

"Why?"

"Because you'll die from an ulcer first."

"You think so?"

"I really do," Ferris said. "But the good news is ulcers can be totally avoided. All you gotta do is relax. And as your best friend I'm going to show you how to enjoy life for what it is. We start today. I'll see you here in fifteen minutes."

Cameron hung up the phone. He knew that what Ferris said was true. Somehow Ferris always managed to put things into a very simple perspective. He made sense in a weird, illogical way. Illogical that was, to everyone except Ferris.

7

SLOANE Petersen opened her locker and quickly checked her hair in the mirror. As she reached for some books, her eye caught the strip of snapshots of Ferris and her that they'd taken together in the photo machine at the mall. Usually that photo made her smile, but today she just pursed her lips and looked away. Ferris, she thought, I can't believe you'd just leave me in this dump. She slammed her locker closed and turned around.

Jeanie Bueller was standing right behind her.

"Aah!" Sloane let out a little shriek. "God, you frightened me."

A half smile appeared on Jeanie's lips. "Sorry," she said.

Sloane caught her breath. "Well, it's nice to see you, Jeanie. Now I've really got to go."

Jeanie pushed her arm against the locker next to Sloane's, blocking her path. "Wait," she said. "I want to know what's going on."

"What's going on with what?"

Jeanie squinted at her. "Don't give me that Little Miss Innocent crap. You know what my brother's up to."

Sloane shrugged. "No, I don't know. All you told me was that he was ditching."

"Listen," Jeanie said. "In the last five minutes at least twenty different people have come up and said they were sorry to hear about Ferris. They all think he's on the verge of death. I saw him this morning and he was pulling the biggest fake-o ditch job on my parents you ever saw. Now I know something is going on and I just want you to tell me what it is."

"I'm sorry, Jeanie, but I don't know anything," Sloane said. But she was happy to hear the news. If Ferris was up to something really good, there was a chance he just hadn't gotten in touch with her yet. But he would. Wouldn't he?

Jeanie obviously didn't believe her. "He hasn't had you paged to the pay phone?" she asked. "He hasn't sent a message? You mean to tell me that you don't even know that he's telling people that if he dies he's giving his eyes to Stevie Wonder?"

Sloane forced back a smile and just shook her head.

Jeanie gave her a skeptical look. "If you're lying, I'll find out," she said, threateningly, and then stormed down the hall.

Sloane turned and quickly headed for English class. She was going to be late because of that total nar. As she ran down the hall she wondered how that pinhead and Ferris could have been hatched out of the same womb. It was like Mother Nature had dumped all the good stuff into Ferris and had nothing but jerko genes left when Jeanie came around.

She got to class and took a seat. In the front of the room, old Mr. Clark, the English teacher, had already started his lecture.

"In what way is the author's use of the prison symbolic of the protagonist's struggle and how does this relate to our discussion of the uses of irony?"

Sloane caught her breath and sighed. If she had to

be late, it was a good thing this was the class. Clark looked like a piece of ancient history. He probably hadn't even noticed that she'd been tardy.

Peggy Barnet, a fellow cheerleader and Sloane's best friend in English class, leaned toward her.

"I heard about Ferris," Peggy whispered.

Sloane nodded.

"Are you really devastated?"

"Not yet," Sloane whispered back.

"They say that no one has ever survived halitosis of the brain," Peggy whispered. "I mean, it's so rare I've never even heard of it before."

"Ferris is pretty tough," Sloane whispered back.

"If he dies, what do you think you'll wear to the funeral?"

"My cheerleading uniform with a black armband," Sloane said.

Peggy gasped. "Really?"

Sloane nodded. "That's the way he'd want it."

There was a knock on the door and Mrs. Sparrow, the school nurse, waddled in, looking a little like a large white snowman. She was about five-two and had to weigh at least 220 pounds. A few years before, the football coach had tried to talk her into playing nose tackle after the starting tackle on the team got injured. She'd said okay, but Principal Rooney had nixed the deal as unfair to the opposing team.

Everyone in the classroom watched Mrs. Sparrow waddle directly to Mr. Clark—everyone except Sloane. She was gathering up her books.

The old teacher had to bend over so that she could whisper something in his ear. Mrs. Sparrow's five double chins jiggled and Mr. Clark slowly nodded. Finally, Mrs. Sparrow turned to the class. "Sloane Petersen?"

Sloane sat up straight, aware that the entire class was staring at her.

"May I see you outside for a moment?" Mrs. Sparrow said. "There's been an emergency."

Sloane nodded and turned to Peggy.

"Dead grandmother," she said, and quietly left to join Mrs. Sparrow in the hall. The nurse closed the door and reached for Sloane's hand. It felt like shaking hands with a catcher's mitt. Mrs. Sparrow looked like she was about to cry. "Sloane, I have bad news. Your grandmother has died."

Sloane nodded and looked down at the floor so that the nurse couldn't see her smile. Ferris, she thought, I love you.

The doorbell rang and Ferris went to answer it. Outside, Cameron stood with his pockets bulging with cold medications. He looked unhappy.

"Come on in, man, you're just in time," Ferris said solemnly.

Cameron stepped into the house. "I don't know why I'm here," he said.

"You're here to help me," Ferris said, leading him toward the kitchen.

"Help you?" Cameron said. "But I'm the one who's sick."

"I know, but this will make you feel better," Ferris said. He reached for the kitchen phone and dialed a number.

"What are you doing?" Cameron asked.

"I'm calling Rooney."

"*What!*"

Ferris put his hand over the receiver. "You're Sloane's father. The school knows Sloane's grandmother has died. You're getting Sloane excused from classes. Stay loose, put your heart into it. I'll be in the living room."

Cameron was almost completely overcome by terror. He opened his mouth, but no words came out. Ferris handed him the phone. "Okay, kid, you're on."

In the principal's office Ed Rooney shoved his hands into his suit pockets and scowled.

"Dead grandmother?" he asked in disbelief.

Ms. Vine nodded. "That's what Petersen said. I had Florence Sparrow notify Sloane."

"Wait a minute," Rooney said. "Who's this girl going with?"

"Well, it's really hard to tell these days who is with who," Ms. Vine said. "I mean, it isn't like the old days where we wore the guy's team jacket or his ID bracelet at least."

Rooney nodded impatiently. "Yes, yes, Ms. Vine, I know. You've told me about that before. Now just tell me who *you think* she's going with."

"Well, I do see her a lot with Ferris Bueller."

Recognition flashed through Rooney's mind. He punched several keys on the computer terminal on his desk. Sloane Petersen's statistics came up on the screen. Next to absences was the number eight.

Rooney smiled. "Well, I'll be damned," he mumbled to himself. He looked up at Ms. Vine. "Get me Mr. Petersen's daytime number."

Ms. Vine nodded, but before she could return to her desk, the phone on Mr. Rooney's desk began to ring. "Should I answer it?" she asked.

Rooney nodded.

Ms. Vine reached over and picked up the principal's phone. "Shermer High School, Mr. Rooney's office." A second later she put her hand over the receiver. "Guess what?" she whispered to Rooney. "It's Mr. Petersen."

The principal was startled. Or was it so surprising? He lifted the phone to his ear. "Ed Rooney."

"Ed? This is George Petersen," said a voice that sounded an awful lot like an eighteen-year-old kid trying to sound like a forty-five-year-old man. "It's a very sad day for our family. We've had a bit of bad luck this morning as you may have heard."

Rooney rolled his eyes. "Yes, I heard. Boy, what a blow. Gosh, I'm all broken up."

"It's been a tough morning. We've got a lot of family business to take care of. If you wouldn't mind excusing Sloane."

Just at that moment 0807 began to flash. In the outer office, Ms. Vine answered the phone. A second later she rushed into Rooney's office, her arms waving in the air. Rooney ignored her; he was having too good a time to be interrupted.

"Huh? Oh, sure, I'd be happy to release Sloane. You produce a corpse and I'll release Sloane. I want to see this dead grandmother firsthand."

Ms. Vine went crazy. She pleaded silently with him to put the call on hold. Rooney just looked up at her and smiled. He covered the phone's mouthpiece with his hand and whispered to her, "It's Ferris Bueller. Gutsy little twerp. I'm gonna set a trap and let him walk right into it.

He uncovered the mouthpiece. "That's right. Cart the stiff in and I'll turn over your daughter. It's school policy." Pleased with himself beyond all belief, Rooney smirked. "Was this your mother?" He looked at Ms. Vine knowingly. The woman was still trying to get his attention. Rooney just held up his hand. "I'll tell you what, you don't like my policies, you can just come on down and smooch my big old white butt. You hear me?"

Ms. Vine couldn't stand it any longer. She stamped her foot.

Rooney covered the phone with his hand. "What!?" he asked, annoyed at being interrupted.

"It's Ferris Bueller on line two," she hissed.

Principal Rooney stared at the phone in horror. Then he quickly pushed 0807. "Ferris?"

"Uh, hi, Mr. Rooney," Ferris said in a weak voice. "I'm sorry to have to disturb you at work, but I was wondering if it would be possible for my sister to bring home any assignments from my classes that I may need."

"Ferris, this isn't some kind of trick, is it?" Rooney begged. "You're not on two phones at once, are you?"

"I'm sorry, Mr. Rooney, I don't understand."

"Just a minute," Rooney said. He switched the phone back to the other line. "Are you still there, Mr. Petersen?"

"You're damn right I am, you stupid son-of-a-bitch!" the voice shouted. "How dare you insult me like that. I'll drag your ass before the school board."

"I'll be right back with you, sir," Rooney said meekly. He switched back to Ferris. "Ferris, please, I beg you. Tell me it's you on the other line, please!"

Ferris coughed. "I'm sorry, Mr. Rooney, the only line I'm on is this one."

Oh, mother of God! Rooney thought. "Listen, Ferris, I'll have to get back to you later." He hung up and switched back to Mr. Petersen. "I'm terribly sorry, sir. I'm afraid there's been a mistake. I owe you an apology."

"You're damn straight you owe me an apology!" the voice screamed. "A family member dies and you insult me. What's the matter with you anyway?"

Rooney broke out in a sweat. "I don't know. I thought you were someone else. You have to know that I would never deliberately insult you. I can't begin to tell you how embarrassed I am."

"Pardon my French, but you're an asshole," the voice said.

"Absolutely!" Rooney nodded enthusiastically. "You hit the nail right on the head. I most certainly am."

Cameron was doing a better job than Ferris had anticipated. While his friend was in the kitchen screaming at Rooney, Ferris went upstairs and changed into one of his father's dark suits. He came back down just in time to hear Cameron scream into the phone, "Call me sir, goddamn it . . . That's better."

Ferris smiled and adjusted his cuff links. Cameron saw him and covered the phone with his hand. "I'm scared shitless," he whispered. "What if Rooney guesses my voice?"

"Impossible," Ferris said. "You're doing great."

Cameron sighed and took his hand off the receiver. "I don't have all day to bark at you so I'll make this short and sweet. I want my daughter out in front of the school in ten minutes. By herself. I don't want anyone around . . ."

Ferris leaped forward to get Cameron's attention. In the process he hit him harder than he should have. Cameron quickly covered the phone again. "What?" he asked.

"Out in front by herself?" Ferris whispered hoarsely. "It's too suspicious! He'll think something's up, mor-on. Cover it."

Cameron panicked. He thrust the phone toward Ferris. "You do it."

Ferris waved at him angrily. "Talk!"

Cameron took a deep breath and cleared his throat before uncovering the receiver. "Uh, I changed my mind, fella. You be out in front with her! I wanna have a few words with you!"

Ferris slapped him again. The phone flew out of Cameron's hand and hit the floor with a *clonk!* Both boys scrambled for it. Cameron got it.

"On second thought, I don't have time to talk to you," Cameron said. "We'll get together soon and have lunch." He slammed the phone down and glared at Ferris. "Why'd you hit me?" he shouted.

"Where's your brain?" Ferris shouted back.

"Why'd you hit me?" Cameron demanded again.

"Where's your brain?" Ferris insisted.

"I asked first," Cameron said.

"How can we pick up Sloane if Rooney's going to be there with her?" Ferris yelled.

"I said for her to be there alone and you freaked," Cameron yelled back.

"You're so stupid," Ferris said. "And anyway, I didn't hit you. I lightly slapped you."

"You hit me," Cameron said. "Look, don't ask me to participate in your crap if you don't like the way I do it." He took out a tissue and blew his nose. "I was home, sick. You get me out of bed, make me jeopardize my future, make me do a phony phone call on the principal, a man who could squeeze my nuts into oblivion, and then you deliberately hurt my feelings."

"I didn't *deliberately* hurt your feelings," Ferris said.

"Oh, really?" Cameron asked.

"Yeah, really."

"Hey, Ferris? Have a nice life." Cameron started toward the door.

Ferris sighed. Maybe he had been a little harsh.

The guy was only trying to do his best for a worthy cause. "Hey, Cameron?"

Cameron didn't answer.

"Cameron, I'm sorry," Ferris said. "I didn't mean to lose my temper. It was uncalled for."

Cameron stopped and turned. "You serious?"

Ferris nodded.

Cameron smiled. "Thanks."

"You did screw up though, right?" Ferris said. "Not that it was necessarily all your fault. Right?"

"I knew it!" Cameron said. "I knew it!"

"So to fix this situation," Ferris said, "I'm going to have to ask you for one small favor."

8

CAMERON drove toward his house. Ferris was sitting next to him. On Ferris's lap were his father's tan raincoat and blue tweed hat.

"You were great!" Ferris was saying. "I'd nominate you for an Oscar!"

Cameron was still shaking. He looked pale.

"I'm telling you," Ferris said, "forget science. Your future is in the theater."

"My future is probably in jail at this point." Cameron groaned. Then he pointed a finger at Ferris. "And you, you mollusk, you promised me you wouldn't make me do anything I'd regret. You swore. 'Just come over and hang out,' you said. 'I won't make you do anything.' Then the next thing I know I'm on the phone cursing out Rooney."

"Tell me you didn't enjoy it," Ferris said.

"I'm not going to enjoy it when he figures out that that was me on the phone," Cameron said. "I'm not going to enjoy it when I get suspended for the rest of my life."

As usual, Cameron was taking things too seriously. "Cameron, my friend," Ferris said. "You are a terrific dude, but you worry too much. You're the only guy I know who is actually concerned that when he grows up there may be a critical shortage of strategic metals."

"Well, it's true," Cameron said.

"Who cares if it's true?" Ferris said. "Who even knows what a strategic metal is."

"Cobalt, nickel—"

"Stop," Ferris said. "I really and truly do not want to know. I would prefer to go through life ignorant on this particular subject."

"Well, you were the one who brought it up," Cameron said.

"I know I brought it up," Ferris said. "But the point I was trying to make is that you worry too much. Especially when there's nothing to worry about. That and your neo-Nazi father probably account for ninety-nine percent of why you're so sick all the time. Did I ever tell you about Garth Volbeck?"

"I don't think so."

"Now this is a kid who has something to worry about," Ferris said. "I mean, his family life is so screwed up that even my parents won't let him come over. His mother runs a gas station. His father is dead, and his sister is rumored to be a prostitute."

Cameron glanced over at Ferris.

"It isn't true," Ferris said. "She just puts out so people will hang out with her. Garth also has an older brother in jail whose a registered psycho. I once watched the guy eat a whole bowl of artificial fruit just so he could see what it was like to have his stomach pumped."

A smile flitted across Cameron's lips.

"But how do you think that makes Garth feel?" Ferris asked. "I mean, the guy is so conditioned to grief he doesn't even feel it anymore."

"So what's he up to?" Cameron asked.

Ferris shook his head sadly. "He's gone, man. Gone

from school. Gone from life. His legacy is a gas station. I hate to say it, but my parents may even be justified in banning him at this point."

A few minutes later they drove into Cameron's driveway and parked. Cameron's house looked like a large flat glass box with curtains inside for privacy. Because it was built on a ravine, the front of the house was on level ground, but the back stretched out into the air and stood on stilts. You could walk off the street and through the house to the back and find yourself fifty feet in the air looking down into a small wooded valley with a creek at the bottom.

Next to the house was the garage, which was really another glass box with curtains and large sliding glass doors. Ferris started to get out of the Civic, but Cameron stopped him. "Wait, I've changed my mind," he said. "Maybe we can pick her up in my car. Maybe Rooney won't recognize it."

Ferris ignored him and pushed open the car door, got out, and walked up the driveway. When he got to the garage, he started to pull the sliding glass doors open. Cameron followed him, looking pale and at a complete loss for words. He knew he was fighting a losing battle.

Ferris stared at the red Ferrari. It was unlike any car he had ever seen. He approached it almost reverently, then turned to Cameron with a gleam in his eye.

"Nineteen-sixty-one Ferrari 250 GTS California. Less than a hundred were made. It has a market value of $165,000. My father spent three years restoring it. It is his *joy*, it is his *passion*, it is his *love*."

"It is his *fault* he didn't lock the garage," Ferris said.

Cameron was not amused. "Ferris, my father loves this car more than life itself."

"A man with priorities so far out of whack doesn't deserve such a fine automobile," Ferris said, a look of dismay on his face.

Cameron ignored him. "He never drives it, Ferris. He just rubs it with a diaper. Remember how insane he went when I broke my retainer? That was a piece of *plastic*; this is a Ferrari!"

"I'm sorry, Cameron, but we can't pick up Sloane in your car. Rooney'd never believe Mr. Petersen drives that piece of shit."

"It's not a piece of shit."

"It's a piece of shit. Don't worry about it. I don't even have a piece of shit. I have to envy yours. Look, I'm sorry but there's nothing else we can do."

Cameron tried a different tack. "He knows the mileage, Ferris."

"Horace doesn't trust you?" Ferris asked, mocking surprise.

"Horace doesn't believe in trust."

"All right, look, this is real simple." Ferris put his arm around Cameron's shoulders and in a conspiratorial tone explained his plan. "Whatever miles we put on, we'll take off."

"How?" Cameron asked suspiciously.

"We'll drive home backward." Ferris beamed at his friend, proud of his idea.

Cameron just stared at Ferris in disbelief. Shaking his head, he told Ferris resolutely, "Forget it. I'm putting my foot down, Ferris. You'll have to think of something else. How about if we rent a Cadillac? My treat!" Cameron tried to muster all the enthusiasm he didn't feel at that moment.

Ferris didn't pay any attention to Cameron's urging. He had climbed into the car and was gunning the engine. Cameron had to shout above the din created by the roar of twelve cylinders. "We could call a limo! A nice stretch job with a TV and bar! How about that? I vote for a limo!" Cameron was excited, impressed with his own idea.

But Ferris just remained behind the wheel, staring at the dashboard. The engine's roar drowned out Cameron's plea.

9

SLOAN sat in the school office, waiting. Kids she knew passed outside in the hall. Some waved at her, some did sign language through the glass to ask if she was in trouble. Sloane smiled and nodded back.

Mr. Rooney came out. He seemed pretty unraveled. "Uh, Sloane, your father is going to pick you up in front of the school. I'll walk you to your locker."

Sloane frowned. That's weird, she thought as she got up. They walked down the hall and Sloane stopped at her locker and threw her books in. She was hoping that Rooney would change his mind and disappear.

"Let me say how deeply saddened I am by your loss," the principal said.

Sloane crouched down and pulled a book from the pile at the bottom of her locker, anticipating a sermon. But it didn't come. Rooney had suddenly clammed up. Sloane stood up and saw why. There was someone else standing next to Mr. Rooney. Oh, no! It was the original pinhead herself, Jeanie Bueller.

Jeanie looked at Principal Rooney and then at Sloane. "Got a problem, Sloane?" she asked with a nasty grin on her face.

"Sloane has had a tragedy in her family," Mr. Rooney said sternly. "It's none of your business and I suggest you get to class immediately."

Jeanie frowned and left. Tragedy, my ass, she thought.

Sloane slammed her locker closed. "Thanks, Mr. Rooney."

The principal nodded. "It was nothing, Sloane. That young lady . . . what's-her-name. Uh, I always forget. Anyway, she's always making a nuisance of herself. I don't know what her problem is. Now back to what I was saying. I had a grandmother once. Two actually."

Sloane rolled her eyes.

They reached the school exit, but instead of saying good-bye, the principal followed her out.

"I think that I can wait for him by myself," Sloane said.

"Oh no, your father insisted I wait with you," Rooney said.

What? Sloane thought. Why would Ferris want that? There had to be a mistake. Her brain started to race. She didn't know what was going on. All she knew was that if she didn't get rid of this dork fast, there was a good chance they'd all get nailed.

Rooney was still blabbering. "Man that is born of a woman hath but a short time to live and is full of misery. He cometh up and is cut down like a flower."

They walked outside. Ferris, Sloane thought, you better cometh up with something good.

The Ferrari shot down the highway. Ferris was driving. He was wearing sunglasses. The blue tweed hat was pulled down low on his head, and he was wearing the tan raincoat over the suit. In his mouth was one of Mr. Frye's foul-tasting briar pipes. The seat next to him was empty. Cameron was hunched down in the back in the little space between the seats and the trunk.

"How come it's my dad's car and I'm taking all the risk and I have to ride back here?" Cameron asked.

"I don't have an explanation," Ferris said. "It just feels right."

"It may feel right to you, but it doesn't feel so right to me," Cameron moaned.

Ferris pushed the accelerator down and the car lurched forward, the engine screaming. "Wow, did you know this thing could do sixty-five in second gear?" he asked.

"Ferris, please, I beg you, slow down."

Ferris backed off. The speedometer read fifty-five. The exit to the school was coming up and he down-shifted into first. The engine screamed.

Cameron yelled louder. "Ferris!"

Ferris turned onto Stonevale Street. About a quarter of a mile ahead of them, he could see the school exit and Rooney and Sloane standing outside it. He hit the brakes and slowed down.

"I don't think I can go through with this," Cameron groaned. "My nerves can't take it. Maybe we better abort the mission."

Ferris slowed the car to a crawl.

"Turn around, eject, jettison extra fuel," Cameron mumbled.

"Calm down, Cam," Ferris said. "We've come this far. We're not aborting."

Cameron started to whimper. "What, are you crazy? You're really going through with this? The principal of the school will be standing right out there. If the man was legally blind he'd still see us."

Ferris took a deep breath. "Just stay quiet, Cam. Remember, we have the element of surprise on our side."

"Surprise?" Cameron groaned. "I can't believe you, Ferris. You must be General Custer reincarnated. He probably told his men they had the element of surprise on their side too. We're walking into a massacre."

"We also have a bus on our side."

Ferris maneuvered the Ferrari into the parking lot and alongside a school bus that blocked the car's view from the school's exit. "I can't believe we're doing this," Cameron moaned from the backseat. "It's unbelievable."

"Just hang tight and stay down," Ferris said. "Quit worrying, Cam, this is going to be a blast. Sloane will get a kick out of it."

Ferris got out of the car and walked over to the passenger side. He leaned against the door, arms folded across his chest. The bus pulled away, revealing Rooney and Sloane waiting outside the exit. Rooney was blabbering away to Sloane, who kept glaring from Rooney to the parking lot. She saw the bus pull out and suddenly a smile spread across her face.

Ferris stood forty yards away, grinning from ear to ear. Their eyes met. I love that crazy kid, Sloane thought, ignoring Rooney's incessant chatter.

Just then Rooney followed Sloane's gaze to the Ferrari.

"Sloane, darling," Ferris called in his deepest voice, trying to mimic the voice Cameron had used on the phone earlier. "Hurry along now."

Rooney squinted in the sunlight, trying to see Mr. Petersen.

"Well, I guess that's my dad," Sloane said. "I really appreciate all your warmth and understanding... It's wonderful. Really," she continued hastily.

"My very best to your dad. Don't forget, huh?"

"Yeah, sure," she said, patting Rooney on the shoulder and walking out to the parking lot. She turned once to wave at Rooney.

Ferris opened the door when he saw Sloane approach. She is gorgeous, he thought as she got closer.

"Have you got a kiss for Daddy?" Ferris asked.

"Are you kidding?" Sloane wrapped her arms around his neck and gave him a big kiss. Then she climbed in the car and glanced one last time toward Rooney.

The principal frowned. Something about this just wasn't right. How many girls kissed their fathers so affectionately? No, this was not right. But before he could walk to the car, Ferris popped the clutch. The car shot out of the lot, leaving fifty feet of rubber down Stonevale Street. The principal squinted and swore. He had a feeling Ferris Bueller had just made a huge fool out of him.

In the Ferrari, Sloane burst out laughing. "I don't believe it!" she squealed. "Right in front of Rooney!" She leaned over and kissed Ferris on the cheek.

Ferris pulled off the tweed hat and threw it in the air. He was incredibly relieved.

"You were great!" Sloane said.

Ferris smiled and glanced into the rearview mirror. Principal Rooney was growing smaller and smaller in the distance. "I do believe high school history has been made just now. What do you think, Cam?"

Cameron got up from the floor and sat in the backseat. "I think I'd rather not make any more history for a few weeks."

Sloane turned around in her seat. "Oh, hi, Cam. You comfortable back there?"

"No."

Sloane turned around and ran her finger over the Ferrari's black dashboard. "Where'd you get this fabulous car, Ferris?"

"From me," Cameron said. "And you better enjoy it fast because it's going home. Right, Ferris?"

Ferris nodded.

Sloane leaned back in the seat. "So what are we going to do today?"

"We're gonna take the car home," Cameron said. "Right, Ferris."

Again, Ferris nodded. Then he looked at Sloane, a grin on his face. He reached out to touch her hair. It felt like silk against her shoulders and she looked serenely happy. "The question isn't 'What are we going to do?' The question is 'What *aren't* we going to do?'"

"I know one thing we aren't going to do all day and that's ride around in this car," Cameron said. "Right, Ferris?"

Ferris looked at Sloane. "If you had access to a car like this, would you take it right back home?" Then he grinned. The answer was self-evident.

10

KATIE Bueller was a successful real estate broker. Clients from all over the country who wanted to buy homes in the suburbs around the big city came to her. She showed them homes, helped them arrange financing, she even helped them find movers.

This morning her clients were from Los Angeles. Dr. Hoffman was an obnoxious anesthesiologist. His wife was a prissy interior decorator and their fifteen-year-old son was a bratty-looking punk named Boyd. But they were interested in a $400,000 house. They'd seen it twice and they liked it. Now it was time to go to the Suburban National Bank and talk about financing with a loan officer.

Katie drove them over to the bank in the station wagon. Dr. Hoffman sat next to her. His wife and son sat in the back.

"Boyd, stop playing with that lighter in the car!" Mrs. Hoffman screeched while they waited for a red light. Katie looked in the rearview mirror and saw that Boyd was playing with a BIC lighter that produced a flame about six inches high.

"Eat my dust, Mom," Boyd replied.

Dr. Hoffman turned around. "Show some respect to your mother."

Boyd sneered. "What are ya gonna do, Dad? Anesthetize me?"

It wouldn't be a bad idea, Katie thought.

"I can't believe we're gonna move to the Midwest," Boyd said. "What a wasteland. We've been here three days and I haven't seen a single head-banger. They probably don't even know what heavy metal is here."

"That's enough," Mrs. Hoffman said.

"Aw, go stuff a Tampax up your nose," Boyd said.

Katie Bueller pulled into the parking lot of Suburban National Bank. At times like this she really hated being a real estate broker.

"If anything happens to this car, my life will be worth less than used toilet paper," Cameron yelled in the back of the Ferrari as it flew down the highway. The wind whipped through their hair. Ferris felt great. Something about riding in a convertible always made him feel invulnerable.

"What could happen?" he asked.

"Yeah, Cam," Sloane said, turning around. "Ferris is a good driver. It's not like we're gonna crash or anything."

"Who's talking about crashing?" Cameron said. "If just a tiny pebble flies off the road and puts a microscopic scratch in the paint, I guarantee you my father will see it."

Sloane looked at Ferris. "Seen any tiny pebbles?"

"Thousands," Ferris said.

"Really?" Cameron gasped.

"Listen, Cam," Ferris said. "It's not healthy to live your life in constant fear. It's not healthy to always worry about tomorrow."

"Why not?" Cameron asked.

"Because when you worry about tomorrow it automatically means that tomorrow you're gonna worry about the day after that. And the day after that and the day after that."

"So? What's wrong with that?"

"It means that every day you're not just worrying about the next day, but about the whole future," Ferris said, as he cut in and out of traffic. "And that's a lot. I mean, worrying about the whole future can really make you weird."

Sloane agreed. "If you keep it up, by the time you get to the future you'll be so weirded out that you won't even be able to enjoy it."

"You think so?" Cameron asked.

Ferris and Sloane both nodded. "Personally," Ferris said, "I've given up worrying completely."

"Yeah, but what about college? And grades? And the SATs and stuff like that?" Cameron asked.

"Listen, Cam," Ferris said. "Did you ever stop to wonder who created college?"

"Uh, no."

"And who created grades?"

"You got me."

"And the SATs?"

"No, I never have wondered about that," Cameron said. "But what's the point?"

"The point is here you are worrying about all this stuff and you don't even know who made it up," Ferris said. "How do you know it even means anything? Maybe it's like algebra. They make you take it in school and then you get out and find out that it's a total joke. Nobody needs algebra for anything. Algebra is like your appendix, totally useless. So how do you know the same isn't true for grades, the SATs, and college? Maybe all that stuff is useless too."

"But what if it isn't?" Cameron asked.

Ferris shrugged. "I'll worry about it then." He pulled

the Ferrari into the parking lot of the Suburban National Bank.

"What are we doing here?" Cameron asked.

"We're picking up supplies," Ferris said.

"You're not going to rob the bank, are you?" Cameron asked.

Ferris innocently looked at him. "Do I look like the kind of person who goes around robbing banks?"

"I don't know," Cameron said. "I don't know what a bank robber looks like."

"From what I've seen," Sloane said, "they look a lot more like you than Ferris."

Cameron looked horrified. "Oh, God. Ferris, you're not going to make me rob the bank, are you?"

Ferris rolled his eyes and got out.

Suburban National was a pretty cool bank, as banks went. The tellers didn't hide behind bulletproof glass or metal grating like they did in some banks. There was orange carpeting on the floor and houseplants and paintings on the wall. Everybody was out in the open where you could see them. Whoever designed the bank must have figured that people would feel more comfortable if they thought they were in their living rooms.

The three kids walked in and headed for the teller windows. To their right loan officers were sitting at their desks conducting business. To their left was a long wooden countertop with pens on chains, deposit slips, and IRA applications.

They went up to a woman teller in her early seventies, who would have been a pleasant-looking woman, except that she wore her silver-blue hair in a tall, stiff-looking beehive hairdo that reminded Ferris of the learning tower of Pisa.

When she saw him, she smiled. "Why Ferris, how nice to see you again."

"Hi, Mrs. Froehling, how are you?" Ferris said, leaning into the teller's window.

Mrs. Froehling reached up to her ear to adjust her hearing aid. "I'm sorry, dear, what did you say?"

"I asked how you were," Ferris said.

"Oh, well, my arm is still a little stiff," the old teller said. "You remember I broke it some time back."

Ferris nodded sympathetically. "I'm really sorry to hear that. I guess it kind of kills your chances with the Cubs this year, huh?"

The teller scowled a little. "I'm sorry dear, what did you say?"

"I said your hair really looks gorgeous," Ferris said.

Mrs. Froehling smiled and patted the beehive. "I've worn it this way for ages."

Ferris pretended to be shocked. "Really? But it looks so contemporary. How about that?" Then he took out a savings bond and laid it on the counter. "Anyway, I'd like to cash this."

Mrs. Froehling looked down at the bond. She seemed to be deep in thought. Suddenly she looked up. "You know, it's none of my business, but shouldn't you be in school today?"

Cameron cleared his throat and Ferris quickly jabbed him in the ribs.

"Uh, gee, Mrs. Froehling," he said. "I've been out of school for a couple of years now. In fact, I'm married. This is my wife, uh...Madonna."

Sloane smiled. "Delighted to meet you, Mrs. Froehling."

Ferris pointed to Cameron. "And this is my brother-in-law, ZZ Top. ZZ, this is my favorite bank teller in the whole wide world, Mrs. Froehling."

Cameron sighed. "It's a pleasure."

"Did you say Top?" the old teller asked.

"Yeah," Cameron said.

"You don't have an uncle in St. Louis, do you?"

"Uh, uh..." Cameron wasn't sure what to say.

Ferris nudged him. "Oh, she must mean old Pop Top. Your uncle who worked in the brewery."

"Oh, right," Cameron said.

"Isn't Top a Slavic name?" Mrs. Froehling asked him.

"Yeah," Cameron said. "It comes from Toppalloppacis."

Mrs. Froehling started to adjust her hearing aid again. Ferris was growing impatient. The world outside was waiting.

"See," he cut in, "the reason I need to cash this bond in is we're gonna have a baby and we need money for a crib, food pellets, leash, and a water dish."

Mrs. Froehling turned to Sloane. "A baby! You must be so excited."

"Oh, I'm just thrilled," Sloane said. "I really can't wait to wear those jeans with the stretch panel in the front."

Mrs. Froehling nodded and leaned forward over the counter. "And you're hardly showing at all."

"We just conceived last night," Ferris said. He put his arm around Sloane, drawing her near for a moment.

The old teller scowled a little. "Oh, uh, I see. And are you hoping for a boy or a girl?"

"Actually we're hoping for a Jeep," Sloane said.

Mrs. Froehling smiled. "That's nice." Her hearing aid was definitely on the fritz.

"Now about this bond," Ferris said.

Cameron looked away while Ferris conned the old teller. God, the guy was unbelievable. He could probably talk the pope into converting to Judaism. He gazed around the bank until something caught his eye. A bunch of people were sitting around one of the loan officers' desks and among them was a kid with a Mohawk haircut. Two of the adults were strangers, but the lady in the gray suit looked awfully familiar. Cameron squinted. No, it couldn't be. He squinted some more. Holy crap!

He quickly turned to Ferris and tugged at his shirt.

"Not now," Ferris whispered as he watched Mrs. Froehling inspect the bond. The moment was critical.

"But Ferris!" Cameron hissed.

"Cool out, man," Ferris whispered back. Then he turned again to Mrs. Froehling. "I'm sure you'll find everything in order."

"Things may be in order over here," Cameron whispered. "But they're really out of order over by the loan officer's desk."

Ferris turned and looked at Cameron as if he was out of his gourd. Then he looked over at the loan officer's desk. Whoa! Could that really be his mother? It took him a second to recognize the enormity of the coincidence. He blinked and then turned stiffly back to the teller.

Mrs. Froehling was pointing a bony finger at the bond. "Now, Ferris, if you cash this bond, you're going to have to pay an early withdrawal penalty. You'd be better off waiting three years until it matures."

"I understand that, Mrs. Froehling," Ferris said hastily. "Unfortunately it doesn't look like the little tyke is going to stay in the oven that long. Also, uh, I just realized we're running a little late."

Sloane had just noticed Mrs. Bueller too. "Uh, we have to go to the store to pick baby names before they're all taken."

"We gotta get out of here!" Cameron whispered.

"But you see," Mrs. Froehling said, "it's silly to

cash in a bond that isn't mature. If you'd just hold on to it..."

Ferris kept glancing over at his mother, less than fifty feet away. What an unbelievable stroke of bad luck!

"Really, Mrs. Froehling," he said quickly. "I'm completely aware of the consequences."

"You're throwing away four dollars," the teller said.

"We gotta get out of here!" Cameron whispered again.

"Uh, not throwing it away, ma'am," Ferris said. "I'm giving it to the government. They need it. Do you know what an aircraft carrier goes for these days?"

"A what?" Mrs. Froehling said.

"Could you just cash it, please?" Ferris asked.

The old teller relented and a minute later Ferris had the cash. He and the others dashed through the side door. They ran across the parking lot and jumped into the Ferrari.

"I can't believe it," Cameron gasped as Ferris stuck the key in the ignition and started up the car. "Of all the banks in the world, she picks this one."

Sloane sighed. "Well, we made it."

"Yeah," Ferris said, steering the car out of the parking lot. "Remind me to send Mrs. Froehling a baby announcement. 'We are proud to announce the birth of our Jeep.'"

They all laughed. Ferris steered the car onto the street. Cameron abruptly stopped laughing.

"Uh, Ferris," he said. "My house is in the other direction."

"I know," Ferris said.

Cameron was quiet for a moment. Then he said in a resigned tone, "We're heading for the city."

"It's a great place," Sloane said.

Cameron looked glum.

"What could happen in the city?" Ferris asked.

"It could get dented," Cameron said. "It could get hit by another car, it could get stolen, the radio could be ripped off, the tires slashed, the windshield broken."

Sloane turned and looked at him. "Cam, you always look at the dark side of things."

Cameron sighed. "It's my nature."

The meeting with Mr. Haupt at the bank was mercifully short. Dr. Hoffman was apparently quite good at putting people to sleep and his financial statement was a triple-A. Katie Bueller was pleased. Now all she had to do was take them back to the house for one last look.

As she and the Hoffmans got up to leave the bank, that funny old teller with the beehive hairdo stopped her. "Oh, Mrs. Bueller, how are you?"

"Just fine, Mrs. Froehling. And you?"

"Well, my elbow still gives me the dickens," Mrs. Froehling said, rubbing it. "Say, congratulations."

Katie looked at her blankly. She usually stopped to chat with the older woman, but today her patience was running short and she wanted to get rid of the Hoffmans as soon as possible. So she just smiled politely.

"And I just met Madonna," the old lady said, patting her on the arm. "You can hardly tell. And on such a slim girl too. Well, keep me posted. I'll want to send a gift."

Katie Bueller just nodded, humoring the woman. Mrs. Froehling had always been a little strange, but now she was babbling nonsense. Katie hoped she was getting close to retirement.

11

ROONEY could not shake the scene from his thoughts. He'd been had in broad daylight. Ferris Bueller had literally snatched Sloane right out from under him.

Rooney smashed his hand against his desk. By tomorrow the whole school would know. He'd be the laughingstock of the entire student population. His authority would vanish. Kids would start cutting left and right. Anarchy would set in!

Rooney jumped up and started pacing around the office. Bueller had to be brought to justice. No student could be allowed to make such a mockery of the administration. He would have to make Bueller an example for the rest of the students.

The principal pushed down the intercom button and summoned Ms. Vine into the room.

"Yes, Mr. Rooney?"

"I want you to get me the Petersens' home phone number."

Ms. Vine gave him a look. "Back on the trail of Ferris Bueller?"

Rooney glared at her. "Go soak your head. Ferris Bueller's behind this. There's no doubt in my mind. And now he's got Sloane Petersen involved in this thing."

"And her grandmother too," the secretary said, and left.

Rooney sighed. "Dodo."

Ms. Vine went to her desk and looked up the number. A few moments later 0807 on Rooney's phone lit up. Rooney picked up the receiver and listened to it ring.

It was answered by an answering machine: *Hi, this is the Petersen residence. I'm sorry we can't come to the phone right now, but a member of the family has kicked off. If you need to reach us, we'll be at 679-8050.*

Kicked off? Rooney thought as he scribbled down the number. He dialed it and got yet another recording: *Hello, you have just reached the Coughlin Brothers Mortuary. We are unable to come to the phone right now but if you'll leave your name and number...*

Rooney slammed the phone down just as Ms. Vine ran back into his office. "Take this number," the principal yelled, ripping the piece of paper off the notepad. "Look up Coughlin Brothers Mortuary in the phone book and see if this is the number."

Ms. Vine grabbed the number and left. Principal Rooney turned and looked out the window. His jaw tightened. It's me against you, Bueller, he thought, in a fight to the finish.

Ms. Vine was back a few moments later. "The number checks out."

The pencil in Rooney's hand snapped in half.

"Something's going on, goddamn it."

Ms. Vine put the piece of notepaper on his desk. "I don't mean to be impertinent, sir, but there's something I don't understand. There are dozens of kids absent from school every day. Sometimes we know that a few of them are cutting. Why are you so fixated on Ferris?"

Principal Rooney squinted at her. "Because he's dangerous, Ms. Vine. He glorifies cutting class. He is insubordinate and disrespectful and he gives good kids bad ideas. If he succeeds today and the word gets back to the student body, we'll have fifteen hundred Ferris Bueller disciples running around the halls smiling at teachers and screwing them behind their backs."

"He's very popular, Ed. Sportos, motorheads, geeks, sluts ... they all love him."

Rooney sat up and pointed a finger at her. "And that's why I have to catch him," he shouted. "To set an example for these kids. To show them that being a sweetheart like Ferris Bueller is a first-class ticket to nowhere."

Rooney sprang from his desk and grabbed his raincoat. "It's going to stop! I'm gonna catch this kid and I'm gonna put one helluva dent in his future. Fifteen years from now when he looks at the ruin his life's become, he's going to remember Ed Rooney."

Grace Vine watched the principal head for the door. She called after him: "Don't count your chickens till the eggs hatch, Ed."

Jeanie Bueller walked toward gym, thinking about how unfair life had been to her. For as long as she could remember, she had always been Ferris Bueller's sister, what's-her-face.

"Yo!" A voice in the hall snapped her out of her thoughts. A kid in tattered jeans and a Motley Crue T-shirt was standing in front of her holding out a jar with a white piece of paper pasted on the front. It read: *Save Ferris Buller.*

"We're collecting money to help buy Ferris Buller a new kidney," the kid said.

Jeanie stopped and stared at him. She couldn't believe it. How did her brother pull it off?

The kid kept on talking. "Like these kidneys go for about fifty G's these days so every contribution—"

"It's not Buller, you cretin," Jeanie said. "It's Bueller. With an e."

The kid looked at the jar. "Oh, wow, thanks for telling me. Like I'm new in school so I didn't know." He took out a pen and corrected the spelling.

Jeanie's jaw dropped. "You don't even know him."

"So? I've heard of him and he's supposed to be a pretty cool dude," the kid said. "And anyway, what's important is he needs a kidney."

"Well, suppose it was his sister," Jeanie said. "Would you work as hard for a new kidney for her?"

"You mean, for what's-her-face?"

A blinding fury suddenly raged up in Jeanie. "Go piss up a flagpole."

"What?" the kid said.

"Shove it." Jeanie started to walk around him.

"Hey, babe, where's your sense of charity, huh?" the kid asked. "You just want to let a dude like Ferris croak 'cause you can't spare a little dough? Just wait. Someday you may need a favor from Ferris Bueller. Then where'll you be?"

Jeanie didn't answer him. She just walked straight to the gym, thinking only about how much she'd love to kill her brother. *You see, your honor, I really loved my Ferris. I just could not allow him to live such a dishonest life. Everything came so easily to him while the rest of us had to struggle. Don't you understand?*

Of course, I do. Case dismissed.

When she got to the locker room, her friend Sharon

was already there, changing into her field-hockey uniform. Sharon was sort of a misfit. She was about six feet tall and had more of a mustache than some of the boys in their class. And even though she was big, she wasn't coordinated or anything that would make her good in sports. She was just a dork. But then, all of Jeanie's friends were weirdos and dorks.

"Hi, Jeanie," Sharon said. "How's Ferris feeling?"

"I'm going to kill that turd," Jeanie said. She pulled her locker door open so hard that it banged against the one next to it and slammed closed again.

"Why?" Sharon asked. "I heard he was dying."

Jeanie laughed. "If he's dying, I'm Bruce Springsteen. He's such a faker. He manipulates my parents, he does whatever he pleases, whenever he pleases, and he never gets nailed." She finished tying her sneakers. "Well, babe, today I'm the hammer."

Sharon pulled on her athletic jersey. She wore a man's size large. "I don't understand why you're so mad at him. I always thought he was cute."

Jeanie stared at her. "Well, it's an accepted fact that you have no taste. Ferris is not cute. He is not charming, wonderful, or even nice. He is an ignorant mule and the sooner everybody in this school realizes that, the better off we'll be."

"But he seems so sweet," Sharon said. "I mean, he's even nice to me," Sharon said dreamily.

"But don't you see?" Jeanie said. "It's just an act. He strokes you so you sympathize with him."

"It's just nice that he's nice," Sharon said.

Jeanie felt like tearing her hair out. "Are you serious?"

"Sure," Sharon said.

"Let me tell you something," Jeanie said. "I study hard. I work hard. I'm polite and considerate and friendly to all kinds of people. Except morons. I try to be everything a good, decent person should be, and you know what?"

"Everyone thinks you're a bitch," Sharon said.

Jeanie's jaw dropped. "Excuse me?"

Sharon shrugged. "Well, I mean, I don't think you're a bitch, Jeanie."

"Who does?" Jeanie asked. "Rachel?"

"Well..." Sharon smiled nervously. She lifted her shoulders in half acknowledgment.

"Rachel's a dirt-bag. Who else?"

"I don't know," Sharon said. "Just forget it."

Jeanie stared at her gym locker. "Just forget that everybody thinks I'm a bitch? Would you like everybody to think you're a bitch?"

"Not *everybody* thinks you're a bitch," Sharon said.

Jeanie couldn't get over this revelation. "Do you mean to tell me that all the time you've known me, you've known that everyone else thinks I'm a bitch?"

"Well, it's not like they all think *I'm* so wonderful," Sharon said.

Jeanie nodded. "Maybe everybody would be happier if I were to die in a flaming car accident or something."

"Or maybe if you didn't act like such a bitch..." Sharon started to say.

Jeanie turned and stared at her. "Am I acting like a bitch?"

"I didn't mean it that way," Sharon said.

"Is this some kind of conspiracy to dump all over me or something?" Jeanie suddenly asked. "Is my brother behind this? I'll bet he gets pleasure from making me look like a bitch. I'll bet he does it on purpose. Tell me he told you to say this"—Jeanie made a fist—"Tell me the truth or I'll pinch your face."

Sharon stared back at her for a long time. "I think the truth is you really have a problem, Jeanie."

"Me? I have a problem?"

"Somebody who threatens to pinch a person's face has a problem," Sharon said.

"All right. How about if I punch you in the face?" Jeanie said.

Sharon got up. "Take a walk, Jeanie."

"Where are you going?" Jeanie asked.

"I've changed my mind," Sharon said. "Maybe I do think you're a bitch."

"Oh yeah? I'm having a bad day. If you walk out of here you lose a friend." Jeanie screamed at her.

Sharon just walked away.

"And if it means anything to you," Jeanie screamed. "I have my period! My body's ridding itself of old eggs, goddamn it!"

But Sharon was gone. Jeanie swung around and kicked her locker as hard as she could. Ferris, she thought, I know you're behind this. You're gone. You're monkey's meat.

12

FERRIS steered the Ferrari down Lake Shore Drive. Inside, a Pink Floyd song was blasting out of the Blaupunkt. Next to him, Sloane was tapping her fingers against her knee to the beat and gazing up at the Chicago skyline with a smile on her face. In the back, Cameron was scrunched up and looking a bit ill.

Ferris was driving at sixty-five miles per hour, pointing to various buildings as they passed. Every once in a while he'd turn to Cameron in the backseat to describe one of the sights, but Cameron would go so crazy that Ferris would turn back to the wheel. He felt great—nothing could hurt him. He wished Cameron would lighten up.

Ferris turned the volume down a little. "Before my grandfather kicked, he once told me that a rich man who lives like a poor man is poor, and a poor man who lives like a rich man is rich."

"Until he gets caught," Cameron mumbled.

Sloane glanced at Ferris and rolled her eyes.

"I mean," Cameron continued, "I can't believe you cashed that bond that was supposed to be for your education."

Ferris gestured at the skyline. "But this is my education. An education in life."

Sloane nodded. "And when it's time for an education in lunch, I know a great little French restaurant."

They pulled into a parking garage near the Sears Tower. Ferris and Sloane started to get out.

"What are you doing?" Cameron asked.

"We're getting out," Ferris said.

"You can't leave this car here," said Cameron.

"Why not, Cam?" Sloane asked.

"Because something could happen to it."

"What could happen?" Ferris asked.

Cameron started counting on his fingers. "It could get stolen, wrecked, scratched, breathed on wrong. A pigeon could shit on it, who knows?"

"Okay, I'll give the guy a five to watch it," Ferris said.

"What guy?" Cameron asked, looking around.

Out of the office stepped a man wearing a parking garage uniform. He looked about seven feet tall and vaguely human.

"Oh, God," Cameron whimpered.

"You speak English?" Ferris asked.

"Da." The parking attendant had shoulder-length hair, gold teeth, and a goatee.

Ferris slipped him a five-dollar bill. "I want you to take extra special care of this vehicle, okay?"

The parking attendant nodded and carefully opened the car door. He slid gently into the seat and drove away very slowly.

"I don't trust this, Ferris," Cameron said.

Ferris slapped him on the back. "Have some faith, huh? In the context of the history of the universe our leaving a Ferrari at this garage today means practically nothing."

As they walked out to the sidewalk, the parking

attendant signaled to his friend. They both ran their hands along the top of the Ferrari.

Back when he'd been in the Illinois State Penitentiary, Igor Puggha had spent a lot of time reading car magazines. With no women around, cars had become the object of his lust, especially fast red Italian cars. He got into the Ferrari and sat behind the wheel. It was too good to be true. Sam White climbed into the passenger seat, and Igor gunned the engine. The Ferrari shot down Michigan Avenue in the opposite direction from Ferris, Sloane, and Cameron.

"What a mutha!" Sam shouted.

Igor gripped the leather-lined steering wheel and grinned. "Da," he grunted. "Da."

From the street the Sears Tower seemed to rise endlessly into the sky. City traffic rolled past and pedestrians hurried along the sidewalk. Ferris took a deep breath of the carbon-monoxide-laced air.

"Okay, great," Cameron said. "Here we are downtown. What an accomplishment. Now what are we going to do?"

"We could do some shopping," Sloane said.

"No," Ferris said. He pointed to the top of the tower. "We're going up!"

"Why?" Cameron asked.

"Why?" Ferris echoed. "Why did Hillary climb Everest? Why did Columbus sail for India? Because it's there, that's why."

Sloane clutched her heart dramatically. "Take me with you!"

Cameron watched the two of them cross the street in the middle of traffic, nearly getting hit by three different cars. He shook his head. "And I thought I was sick," he said to himself.

Ferris led them into the lobby of the great building,

past the big red and black Calder mobile, past the groups of Japanese tourists, to the express elevator to the observation deck. A bunch of Japanese tourists got in the elevator also, squeezing them to the back. The elevator doors closed and they rocketed upward.

"Do we have to do this?" Cameron asked.

"We don't have to do anything," Ferris said. "We could just dig holes for ourselves and lie down in them and die."

"Or emerge as adults," Sloane said.

Ferris shivered at the thought. "God, a fate even worse than death."

"I don't know," Cameron said. "I always thought it would be kind of cool to be an adult. Then you could push your kids around and they couldn't do anything about it."

Ferris put his arm on Cameron's shoulder. "My friend," he said in a somber voice, "I am beginning to think you are an abused child."

The elevator let them out at the 103rd-floor observation deck. Jabbering excitedly, the Japanese tourists immediately headed for the thick picture windows that rose from the floor to the ceiling on all four sides of the deck. Ferris, Sloane, and Cameron followed them to the windows and looked out. Far below them the city gradually spread away in every direction, turning into suburbs and then farmland.

The tourists seemed really excited by the view.

"I guess you can't get this high in Japan," Sloane said.

"Oh yeah?" Cameron said. "I bet you never tried sake."

Ferris stared at him.

"What is it?" Cameron asked.

Ferris stepped forward and put his hand on his friend's forehead. "Maybe you really are sick."

"Why?" Cameron asked.

"You said something funny."

Cameron pushed him away. "Oh, screw off."

Ferris stood by the window. "You can see four states," he said. "Illinois, Michigan, Wisconsin, and my personal favorite, Indiana."

Cameron seemed to sway a little. "I think I have vertigo."

"If you have to go, use the men's room," Ferris said.

"No, vertigo," Cameron said. "You know, height sickness."

Sloane looked at him. "You're not tall enough to have height sickness."

Cameron sighed. "I can't believe you guys are my friends."

"Neither can we," Ferris said. "Now check this out. Take a step up on this rail. Now lean forward and put your forehead on the glass."

The three of them did it. The glass felt cold against Ferris's forehead, but in that position he could see almost straight down. The sight was dizzying. The streets below looked like the little grooves in a tile floor. The cars and buses looked like tiny bugs. People were infinitesimal dots, barely visible.

On Ferris's right, Cameron looked pale. If he didn't have vertigo before, he sure had it now. "Ferris," he whispered with eyes wide. "I think I see my dad."

Ferris looked at Cameron in disbelief. The poor guy is so terrified he's hallucinating.

"How many schools are out there?" Sloane asked. "And how many kids in those schools wish they were doing something like this instead of sitting listening to some dumb teacher talk about some dumb subject they'll never need to know about?"

"School's not so bad," Ferris said.

Cameron stared at him. "Then what are we doing here?"

"Just taking a day to explore alternative possibilities," Ferris said.

"And what about the other eight days we've ditched this semester?" Sloane asked.

Ferris shrugged. "I guess there have been a lot of alternatives to explore lately."

Cameron and Sloane both shook their heads and turned to watch the tourists, but Ferris continued to look down. One hundred and three stories below a small red dot of a car suddenly shot through traffic.

13

THEY hit the Chicago Mercantile Exchange next. Guys in blue and red coats were running back and forth through the doors, and inside the traders jammed the exchange floor. Ferris, Cameron, and Sloane climbed to the visitors' gallery above the exchange and looked down. From their viewpoint, the traders looked like madmen, waving their arms and screaming frantically.

"My father knows a guy who makes over a million dollars a year doing that," Cameron said.

"How is it that just fifty miles from here there are farmers working their asses off from dawn to dusk and they're going broke while these guys act like jerks for six hours a day and get rich?" Ferris asked.

"I don't know," Sloane said. "But there's something fascinating about this. I feel like we're watching something that doesn't occur anyplace else in the world. It's like the strange mating ritual of some rare species of animal that only exists in a tiny jungle in Peru."

They watched for several minutes. Then Ferris noticed that Sloane had turned and was gazing at him. He smiled back at her. He reached toward her and touched her hair. "Did anyone ever tell you you were beautiful?"

Matthew Broderick stars as Ferris Bueller, a high school senior who makes Chicago his playground on a day off from school, using the philosophy, "Life moves pretty fast. If you don't stop once in a while and look around, you could miss it."

Jennifer Grey as Jeanie Bueller: "You're really letting him stay home? I can't believe this. If I was bleeding out my eyes, you'd make *me* go to school. It's so unfair."

Tom Bueller (*Lyman Ward*): "What's the matter with Ferris?" Joyce Bueller (*Cindy Pickett*): "He doesn't have a fever. But he says his stomach hurts and he's seeing spots."

"You have to plan things out before you take a day off."

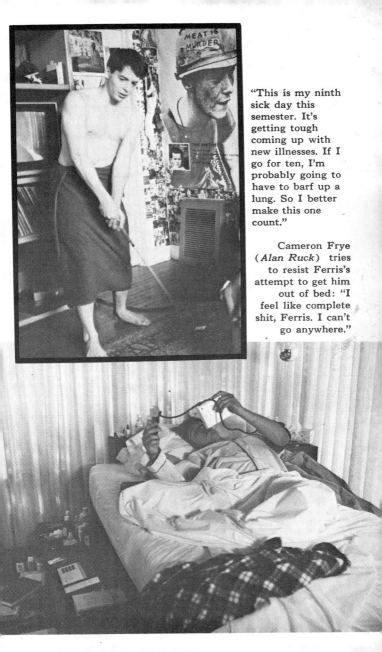

"This is my ninth sick day this semester. It's getting tough coming up with new illnesses. If I go for ten, I'm probably going to have to barf up a lung. So I better make this one count."

Cameron Frye (*Alan Ruck*) tries to resist Ferris's attempt to get him out of bed: "I feel like complete shit, Ferris. I can't go anywhere."

Ferris has the time of his life driving Mr. Frye's 1961 Ferrari 250 GTS California—but Cameron is too nervous to enjoy the ride: "Ferris, my father loves this car more than life itself."

Ferris: "Would you want to get married? I mean if I wasn't a fool."
Sloane (*Mia Sara*): "Sure."
Ferris: "Today?"

Ferris jumps onto a float at the German-American Appreciation Day Parade, captures the crowd's spirit, and spreads his enthusiasm.

The kids are caught in traffic with Mr. Bueller only a foot away. They quickly hide on the floor of the back seat while Sloane keeps an eye on Tom Bueller.

ABOVE: Ferris looks on while Cameron sits in a near catatonic state: "My best friend has flipped out. Conventional wisdom would suggest a trip to the nearest trauma center. *I* think this calls for something bold, something wet, something wild."

LEFT: Mr. Rooney (*Jeffrey Jones*), the principal, peers through the Buellers' windows in hopes of catching Ferris in the act of truancy.

RIGHT: Ferris careens wildly through backyards to make it home before his parents.

BELOW: In a final confrontation with Principal Rooney, Ferris needs all the help he can get . . . but is Jeanie the rescuer he's looking for?

Sloane nodded. "Yes, everyone."

"How many said they loved you?" Ferris asked.

"Plenty."

"Did you believe them?"

Sloane shook her head. "Do you love me? she asked.

"Do you love me?" Ferris asked back.

"I asked first," Sloane said.

Ferris leaned back and tried to think of a good answer. "Would I trash a day of education to be with you if I didn't love you?"

"Yes," Sloane said.

"Would I risk damaging a deep and wonderfully enriching relationship with my parents if I didn't love you?" he asked.

"Yes." She giggled.

"Well, I love you anyway," Ferris said, putting his arm around her.

Sloane leaned forward and kissed him.

"Would you marry me?" Ferris asked. "I mean, if I wasn't a fool?"

"Sure," Sloane said.

"Today?" Ferris asked.

Sloane gave him a look.

"Hey, I'm serious," Ferris said.

"I can't believe I'm a witness to this," Cameron groaned.

"Really," Ferris said. "I'll do it today if you will."

"I hate to burst your bubble," Cameron said, "but you need a blood test. If your blood's not compatible, you could produce a cabbage. So the state requires a blood test."

"Okay," Ferris said.

"And you have to wait twenty-four hours," Cameron said.

"Okay," Ferris said.

"Wait, I'm not getting married," Sloane said.

"Why not?" Ferris asked.

"What do you mean, why not?" she said. "Think about it."

"Okay," Ferris said. "Besides being too young and your stepfather hating my guts and us not having anyplace to live and you feeling awkward about being the only cheerleader with a husband, give me one good reason why we shouldn't."

"I can give you two," Cameron said. "My mother and my father."

Ferris looked at him. "They don't want me to marry Sloane?"

"No, dummy, they're two good reasons not to get married," Cameron said. "They're married and they hate each other."

"Yeah, but they're old," Ferris said. "They're too freaked out about what happened to their bodies to remember whether or not they're in love. And besides, your father is a neo-Nazi toad and your mother is wired out. So it's understandable."

"You think that it's understandable that he hates his wife and kid and is in love with a Ferrari?" Cameron asked.

"So maybe they should get divorced," Sloane said. "My parents got divorced. It happens ten thousand times a day."

"Just because it happens doesn't make it right," Cameron said. "I mean, how does it make you feel? Are you really comfortable with it?"

Sloane shrugged and the corners of her mouth turned down. "It's not something you can get comfortable with, but you live with it. I mean, my parents are human, too, right? They're not perfect. My father gave up his whole family for a twenty-five-year-old secretary in his company. None of us had the slightest inkling of what was going on and then all of a sudden one day he came home and said he was moving out. Just like that."

Ferris's expression belied his thoughts. He didn't think he'd ever seen Sloane sad before, and compassion welled up inside of him. "You never told me that," he said.

"It's not something I broadcast," Sloane said. "I guess the thing that blew me away was that it was pure selfishness on his part. He just dumped me and my brother and my mother and split. Up to that point in his life he'd never done a single selfish thing. Looking back at it, I guess it was kind of unnatural. Like he only lived to make the rest of his family happy. And all the while this thing was building up inside of him, like this need to do something for himself. And then bang! It just all came out. And the next day he was gone."

Ferris shook his head. "I can't imagine my old man doing that, but I guess it's possible."

Cameron nodded. "My old man did it years ago. Except he didn't have to get divorced."

"What do you mean?" Ferris asked.

"Well, Sloane's father divorced her mother because it's not socially acceptable to live with your wife and be in love with your secretary at the same time," Cameron said. "But society sees nothing wrong with living with your wife and being in love with your Ferrari."

"It does make you think," Sloane said. "I mean, I used to think that when I had a kid, I wouldn't care how much I wanted to do something. If it was gonna screw up the kid, I wouldn't do it. But you can't stop being human."

"Why don't you go talk to your old man," Cameron said. "I mean, tell him you think it was a really selfish thing to do and that you and your brother and mom still need him."

"Why should he listen to me?" Sloane asked. "I don't know what his life was like. Maybe he was really unhappy for a long time. Besides, to him I'm just a kid. As long as you live in your parents' house, they call the shots. You want to call the shots? You have to move out."

"You're saying I should run away?" Cameron asked.

"No," Ferris said, getting up. "She's saying it's time for lunch."

"What?" said Sloane.

Ferris offered his hand and helped her up. "Come on, let's feed Cameron."

They started out of the visitors' gallery, but just before they reached the door, Ferris had an inspiration. He ran back, looked down at the exchange floor, cupped his hands around his mouth, and shouted, *"BUY!"*

14

THEY went to the fancy French restaurant Sloane told them about. It was filled with potted palms, tasteful china, and soft music played in the background. Most of the clientele were business people in suits or elegant women lunching with friends. Next to their carefully groomed appearances, Ferris's T-shirt and leather jacket stood out, but he didn't seem to notice. He stood by a desk near the front, waiting for the maître d' to seat him, Sloane, and Cameron. A huge bouquet of fresh flowers spilled onto the desk.

"Aren't they beautiful?" Sloane said.

Ferris nodded. Then he pulled a rose out of the arrangement. "For you, my dear."

Sloane curtsied. "Why, thank you."

Cameron nudged Ferris. "You sure we can afford this place?"

"Sure, no sweat," Ferris said, peeking into the reservation book.

The maître d' arrived at the desk. He was about thirty-five, with slicked-back blond hair and an immaculate gray suit.

"May I help you?" he asked condenscendingly. He'd had to deal with kids like this before.

Ferris acted surprised. "You can sure as hell try.

Hi! I'm Abe Frohman. Party of three for twelve noon."

The maître d' gave him a look.

"Is there a problem?" Ferris asked.

The maître d' cleared his throat. "You're Abe Frohman?"

"I'm Abe Frohman."

"I'm sorry, son," the maître d' said with a chuckle. "I'm very busy right now. If you have trouble finding the door..."

Sloane tugged at Ferris's sleeve, but he ignored her. Who did this guy think he was? "Are you suggesting that I'm not who I say I am?"

"I'm suggesting that you leave before I have to get snooty," the maître d' said.

Cameron nudged him. "Let's go ... Abe."

Ferris shook his head. "I'm not going anywhere." He turned back to the maître d'. "We'd like to be seated."

"If you won't leave of your own accord, I'm afraid I'll have to call the police!"

"Be my guest," Ferris said. Then he had an idea. He quicky grabbed the phone. "Better yet, I'll call them myself."

The maître d' smiled smugly as Ferris punched the numbers on the phone. A second later the restaurant's second line lit up and rang. The maître d' frowned and reached for the phone in Ferris's hand.

Ferris quickly pulled it away. "You touch me and I'll yell 'Rat!' There's another phone around here. Find it."

The maître d' scowled and ran for the other phone. As soon as he was out of sight, Cameron nudged Ferris again.

"Ferris," he said in a low voice. "Let's drop it, please?"

"Cam's right," Sloane said. "We've done enough.

You're gonna go too far and we're gonna get busted."

Ferris shook his head. "A: You can never go too far. And B: If I'm gonna get busted, it's not gonna be by a guy like that." On the phone he heard the maître d' answer from another room. Ferris handed the receiver to Sloane. "Ask for Abe Frohman," he whispered.

On the other end of the phone the maître d's voice mumbled the name of the restaurant and then, *"C'est qui?"*

Sloane's voice sounded quite demure as she asked, "Is Abe Frohman there?"

Certain the woman was speaking of someone entirely different from the punk impersonating Mr. Frohman, he smiled mischievously. "Let me check in the bar—please describe him for me."

"He's wearing a leather jacket, T-shirt, he's devastatingly handsome, and—"

Before Sloane could finish her sentence, the maître d' hung up the phone in stunned disbelief. He was also angry. As he walked back to where Ferris stood, his face turned red with frustration.

Sloane grinned. She had played her part perfectly, and in a minute the maître d' was apologizing and seating them at a table in the corner. A pink tablecloth, sterling silver flatware, and white china spelled elegance. A small crystal vase of flowers stood in the center.

The maître d' helped Sloane with her chair and turned to Ferris. "I appreciate your understanding, Mr. Frohman," he said humbly.

"Don't think twice about it," Ferris said. "Understanding is what makes it possible for people like us to tolerate a person like yourself."

"Thank you," the maître d' said stiffly.

"My pleasure," Ferris said.

"Enjoy your luncheon." The maître d' backed away.

Ferris turned to Sloane and kissed her lightly on the cheek. "Darling, you were wonderful."

"Oh, but I have a wonderful teacher," Sloane replied, batting her eyelashes.

Ferris looked at Cameron. "And you, my friend?"

Cameron just shook his head.

Ferris smiled. "And you thought we wouldn't have any fun. Shame on you."

Sloane looked around the restaurant. "This is beautiful," she whispered, snuggling close to Ferris.

The waiter brought the menu. It was in French.

Sloane looked at the others. "God, I wish one of us knew French."

"You see," Ferris said. "This is a perfect example of what is wrong with school. They never teach you anything relevant. I've been taking French since sixth grade, but do you think they ever taught me anything practical like how to read a menu? Of course not. Instead I'm supposed to memorize a bunch of irregular verbs. You can't eat an irregular verb."

"I smoked one once," Cameron said. "When I came down, I was in Rockford."

Ferris and Sloane stared at him. Before they could say anything, the waiter came back for their orders. Since no one knew what anything on the menu was, they just ordered what sounded interesting. The waiter wrote down their requests and left.

"What's Rockford like?" Sloane asked.

"It's the kind of place that makes you think about suicide," Cameron said. "So I thought about suicide and you know what?"

"You killed yourself and this is a dream," Ferris said.

Cameron shook his head. "I decided that suicide

is a ridiculous thing. And for one simple reason. Want to hear it?"

Sloane nodded.

Cameron leaned over the table toward her. "Suppose time has a beginning and an end," he said.

"But that's impossible," Sloane said. "Time has been going on forever and it will continue to go on forever. It's not connected to anything tangible. It has no beginning and no end. Man just likes to think it does because he's incapable of dealing with infinity."

Ferris gazed at her and grinned. "You know what amazes me about you, Sloane?"

"What?"

"You're the only A-student cheerleader I ever knew who actually thinks and doesn't just spit out data by rote. You are truly a credit to the breed."

Sloane smiled. "Thanks, Ferris."

"Okay, look," Cameron said. "Just for this discussion, let's pretend that time does have a beginning and an end. You could even say that time began a billion years ago and it will end a billion years from now. Okay?"

Ferris and Sloane nodded.

"Now, understand that what I'm about to say is basically an atheist's point of view. I mean, if there is a heaven and after we die we can all go cruising with the angels, then this theory has no merit. Okay?"

Again Ferris and Sloane nodded.

"Right," Cameron said. "Then here's my reasoning. Essentially, between the moment time began and the moment you were born you were dead. I mean, you weren't born yet so you weren't alive and if you're not alive you're dead, right? Okay, so that means that for about the first billion years of time, you were dead. Now you're gonna die sooner or later and once you die you're gonna stay dead for the rest of time. So that means that for the next billion years you're gonna be dead. Now, if you figure that you were already dead for a billion years before you were born and you're gonna be dead for another billion years after you die, that means that you're gonna spend almost all of time dead. I mean, compared to that, the amount of time you're alive is nothing."

"So what does that have to do with suicide?" Ferris asked.

"Well, it's simple," Cameron said. "From a statistical point of view, you spend so much more time dead than alive that you might as well enjoy being alive while you're alive."

Ferris realized that basically he and Cameron had the same philosophy. Except, instead of trying to prove it with mathematical equations, Ferris just lived. If he saw an opportunity, he took it; if he wanted to have fun, he had fun. Statistics and the eventuality of death had nothing to do with it.

Meanwhile Sloane looked up at the ceiling and back down at Cameron. "But, Cam, most people don't think of that when they commit suicide. The only thing they think about is that they're in so much physical or emotional pain that they just want to kill themselves to end it."

Cameron shook his head. "Hey, of all the kids you know, who has the most oppressive home life?"

"You," Ferris said.

"Who is the most miserable?" Cameron asked.

"You," Sloane said.

"If you came to school and heard that someone had done himself in, who would you think of first?" Cameron asked.

"You," Ferris and Sloane said.

"That's right," Cameron said. "And I'll tell you

something, that theory works. It's the only thing that's kept me alive for the last five years."

Ferris didn't know what to say. Fortunately he didn't have much time to dwell on it because the waiter had arrived with a big silver tray carrying their lunch.

What the waiter brought looked interesting. He placed their plates in front of them and wished them a bon appétit. Ferris stuck his nose over the food and took a whiff. It smelled interesting. He cut a little piece off with his fork and brought it to his lips. It tasted interesting.

"What do you think it is?" Cameron asked as he began to eat.

Ferris shrugged. "You got me."

Just at that moment, the maître d' strolled over to them. "Is everything to your satisfaction?"

"It's wonderful," Sloane said, looking up at him. "We're just having a little trouble identifying the food."

The maître d' looked at their plates and smiled. "Why, it appears that you are having sweetbreads."

"And what might that be?" Ferris asked.

"Pancreas."

Cameron and Sloane stopped chewing.

"You mean," Ferris said, "pancreas as in the gland that has important functions in digestion and metabolism?"

The maître d' smiled again and nodded.

Ferris coughed. "You mean the pancreas that secretes a thick, colorless fluid containing digestive enzymes? The home of the world-famous isles of Langerhans?"

"I believe I do, sir," the maître d' said, loving every minute of the kid's impressions.

Cameron and Sloane held their napkins to their

mouths, making spitting noises. Ferris sighed deeply and looked up at the maître d' with a forced smile. "Check, please."

A few minutes later he paid for three expensive and mostly untouched lunches. Sloane and Cameron loaded up on free mints at the reception table, and they headed toward the exit.

"Pancreas." Cameron was still groaning. "I can't believe it!"

"Look at it as a learning experience," Ferris said, pushing open the door and stepping out onto the sidewalk.

"This is one case where ignorance would have been bliss," said Sloane.

"At least ignorance would have tasted better than pancreas," Cameron added.

Ferris took a few steps on the sidewalk and suddenly froze. He could not believe what he was seeing. Cameron and Sloane stopped behind him.

"What is it?" Sloane asked.

Ferris quickly lifted his finger to his lips. Then he pointed across the sidewalk. Standing at the curb with his back to them was his father, talking to two other businessmen.

Ferris and the others quickly backed into the vestibule of the restaurant.

"Four thousand restaurants in the downtown area and I pick the one my father goes to," Ferris whispered.

Cameron started to shake. "All he has to do is turn around and he'll see us," he whispered. "We're gonna get pinched for sure."

"No way, Cameron," Ferris said. "Only the meek get pinched. The bold survive." He looked around quickly. The group of Japanese tourists was coming down the sidewalk, following a tour guide. "Let's go," he whispered.

"Where?" Sloane whispered back.

"Stay low." Ferris grabbed her hand and ducked out the door and into the crowd. Cameron followed.

They eased themselves into the middle of the crowd and walked hunched over. "Excuse please, excuse please," Ferris kept whispering. The tourists didn't seem to care. They were too busy listening to the guide, who was speaking rapidly in Japanese.

Ferris, Sloane, and Cameron stayed in the group for about half a block.

"You won't believe this," Cameron whispered.

"What?" Ferris whispered back.

"Guess who's right behind us?"

Ferris turned and looked. His father and his business buddies were strolling along behind the tourist group, still deep in conversation.

"Uh-oh," Sloane gasped, tugging Ferris's hand.

Ferris quickly turned back to see what she was gasping about. Ahead he saw a big green tour bus. The crowd of tourists was starting to get on it.

"What do we do?" Sloane asked.

"We get on the bus," Ferris whispered back.

"Are you serious?" Cameron whispered.

Ferris looked back. His father was right behind them. "We'll get off as soon as he's gone," he whispered.

They got on the bus and walked straight to the back. Dozens of surprised Oriental eyes watched them. The backseat was empty and Ferris sat down and slid to the window. Outside his father and the other businessmen had stopped on the sidewalk again and were chatting right outside the bus.

Sloane nudged him in the ribs and he turned

around. The Japanese tour guide, a small woman with long black hair, was standing in the bus aisle in front of them. She said something in a language Ferris couldn't understand.

"What did she say?" Ferris whispered. Sloane and Cameron shrugged, but a teenage Oriental kid in the seat in front of them turned around.

"She say you no go on this bus."

Ferris nodded and dug into his pocket. He came up with a ten-dollar bill and handed it to the tour guide, who bowed and said something else they couldn't understand.

Ferris tapped the kid on the shoulder. "What did she say?"

The kid grinned. "She say welcome aboard."

15

IGOR Puggha had once read about a car race that was held in the middle of a little country called Monaco somewhere in Europe. For one day a year, the city called Monte Carlo closed its streets to regular traffic and let the world's fastest and most expensive cars race on them. The world's best drivers came to race and the world's wealthiest people came to watch and go to parties. On cold nights in his jail cell, Igor had been kept warm with dreams of the day he would drive in that race. Now suddenly, flashing through the streets of Chicago, he was there. Traffic on the street came to a halt as he shot past in the Ferrari. People on the sidewalks stopped and gasped. Pretty girls waved. It was a dream come true.

The Ferrari shot past the Museum of Art just seconds before the Japanese tour bus arrived. The tourist group went in past the tall gray columns and through the great stone arches, but Ferris and Sloane stopped at a hot-dog vendor on the street to make up for the lunch they'd missed.

Ferris got two dogs with sauerkraut and a Pepsi. "Don't you want anything?" he asked Cameron.

"Just a can of club soda," the kid said. "My stomach's still a little queasy."

"Of course your stomach is queasy, Cam," Sloane said. "You never eat anything."

Ferris and Sloane gobbled their dogs while Cameron sipped his soda. Then they headed toward the museum.

A group of elementary school kids and their teacher stood in a line at the entrance. Each child held his buddy's hand, and when they walked into the main gallery, Ferris followed holding Sloane's hand. A little girl in a yellow dress looked up at them and giggled. Ferris reached down and picked up her hand. Sloane grabbed Cameron's and soon they had formed a chain, walking from room to room. The little kids were having a better time than if they were listening to their teacher rattle on, and Ferris was having a blast. He loved little kids—they were so carefree and easy to please.

After a while they broke free and stood in front of a Rodin sculpture. Ferris struck a pose similar to the nude bronze male. He couldn't imagine anyone feeling comfortable like that.

"You know, I almost enlisted in the Marines yesterday," Cameron said as they walked down the halls lined with priceless paintings and sculptures.

Ferris stared at him. "I thought you didn't believe in suicide."

"I thought it might be good for me," Cameron said, gazing wistfully at a Picasso. Sloane and Ferris each stood in front of a different Picasso. "You know, I could become one of the few, the strong, the brave. I thought that when I got out, it might help me deal better with life."

"What's wrong with the way you deal with life now?" Sloane asked.

Cameron shrugged. "You mean, what's right with the way I deal with life?"

They sat down on a marble bench in front of the Chagall windows. Ferris finished the last of his Pepsi, crumpled the can in his hand, and stuck it in his pocket. "I think the best way to deal with life at the present moment is to contemplate the beauty of art."

"I agree," Sloane said.

Cameron got up. "Well, I think I'll take a little walk."

"See you later," Ferris said. He tilted his head toward Sloane's shoulder and started to get comfortable. Sloane reached for his hand and their fingers entwined.

"Nice, huh?" he said softly.

"Yes," she replied.

Ferris turned and kissed her.

"Are we really gonna stay here?" a voice asked in the middle of the kiss.

Ferris opened one eye. Cameron had returned and was standing next to them, chewing on a fingernail. Ferris closed his eye again.

"Well, are we?" Cameron asked.

"Did you hear something?" Sloane asked dreamily.

"Must have been a ghost," Ferris mumbled.

"I'm serious, guys," Cameron said. "Maybe you can sit back and make out but I just saw this painting that totally freaked me out. I mean, from a distance it looked like this great picture, but when I got up close, all I saw was a zillion little dots. I mean, it was scary."

"Seurat," Sloane said.

"I don't think so," Cameron said. "But it could be myopia. I'm a little nearsighted."

"No, dummy, she means the dude who painted the picture," Ferris said. "His name was Seurat."

"Sir rot?" Cameron scowled. "What was his wife? Lady Decompose?"

Sloane looked at Ferris and rolled her eyes. Then

she turned to Cameron. "Come on, Cam, this is a beautiful museum, we're expanding our appreciation of art. Why do we have to do anything more?"

"Well, this isn't what I had in mind for today."

"What you had in mind for today was lying in bed feeling sorry for yourself," Ferris said.

"True, but at least it was a comfortable bed and there was stuff to watch on the tube."

"Okay," Ferris said. "We won't stay that long. We'll go as soon as one of us comes up with a good suggestion."

"Let's go play video games," Cameron said.

Sloane sighed. "Give me a break."

"We could go to a magic shop," Cameron said.

"Cam, those are very nerdy suggestions, and definitely beneath a person with your intelligence," Ferris said. "I can only assume that you are making them out of total desperation."

"You're right," Cameron said. "I guess I forgot I was with the cool people. Your idea of a good time is probably taking that dumb sight-seeing boat down the Chicago River."

Ferris looked at him and grinned. "Great idea!"

16

THEY were just in time for the next boat. The three of them sat down in a seat on the deck. Sloane leaned back and rolled up her sleeves to catch a few rays. Next to her Ferris did the same. Only Cameron remained sitting erect.

"Are you guys worried about nuclear war?" he asked.

Ferris stared at him. "Hey, the sun's out, it's a beautiful day, we're traveling down one of America's most scenic polluted waterways and you have to bring up nuclear war?"

"When I was walking around the museum, I saw a sign about it being a civil-defense, air-raid shelter and that made me start to think about it," Cameron said.

"There are eight thousand things you could worry about," Ferris said. "Do you have to bring up nukes?"

"It's kind of a raggy subject, Cam," Sloane said.

"Look, guys, so far today we've talked about school, marriage, and suicide," Cameron said. "These are interesting topics, but they're not things that really affect our lives on a daily basis. Nukes, on the other hand, are with us every day. We wake up every morning with the constant possibility of global destruction."

"You want to know what I think?" Sloane said, her eyes still closed. "I think it's an issue because people need something to worry about. They need a major problem that puts all their petty irritations into some kind of perspective."

"Maybe," Cameron said. "But that still doesn't reduce the threat. It's there and it won't go away. I mean, do you have any idea what nuclear winter is?"

Ferris sighed. "Yeah. Everybody's dead, it's real cold, and the skiing's for shit...Now listen, Cameron, don't tell me you're going to get into this nuclear freeze stuff."

"Yeah, Cam," Sloane said. "My stepfather's always going off about how when he was young he was committed to all these dumb causes. In the old days people used to get religion. Then in the sixties they started getting causes. Now they get herpes."

"Your stepfather is full of it," Ferris said. "All old hippies and peaceniks are full of it."

"He says I'm apathetic because I don't care about anything like he did," Sloane said.

"What does he care about now?" Ferris asked.

"Losing his hair."

"I rest my case," Ferris said.

"What's spooky is they still control everything," Cameron said. "They took over when they were young and they never gave it up."

Ferris looked up at a small white puff of a cloud passing slowly overhead. "One of the most frightening experiences of my young life has been observing my parents and our neighbors playing the baby boom edition of Trivial Pursuit. It's chilling to see people crazed with the minutiae of their pasts."

"It's human nature to like then better than now," Sloane said.

"You know," said Cameron. "This is all very interesting, but I'm hungry."

"An hour ago you wanted to queeb," Ferris said.

"I feel better now."

Ferris gestured toward the river. "Lean over and grab a fish."

Cameron got up and leaned over the railing down at the gray water. Suddenly he turned and looked at Ferris and Sloane. "Hey, what about nuclear winter?"

"What about it?" Ferris said.

"Well, don't you ever think about it? I mean, have you ever wondered what must come after it?"

"Sure," Ferris said. "Nuclear spring."

17

JEANIE Bueller stood outside Mr. Rooney's office debating with herself. It is reprehensible to squeal on your own flesh and blood, she told herself, but it is for his own good. His cavalier attitude will get him into trouble later in life.

She took a step toward the office and then stopped. Stop kidding yourself, Jeanie, she thought. The real truth is it'll continue to piss me off and I'll get so wadded up that it'll cause cervix cancer and he'll ruin my life. Screw him. She went in.

Ms. Vine looked up and saw her come in. "Hi, Jeanie. Who's bothering you today?"

Jeanie frowned. Ms. Vine thought she was smart, but she'd get hers someday too. "Is Mr. Rooney in?"

"I'm sorry," Ms. Vine said. "He's not. Can I help you?"

"I seriously doubt it," Jeanie said. "Know when he'll be back?"

"I don't," Ms. Vine said. "He left the grounds on personal business."

Jeanie shook her head in disgust and left the office. I can't believe this, she thought. How can my brother be so lucky? How did he know that if he cut today and I decided to turn him in, Mr. Rooney wouldn't be there? Her hands clenched at her side. I can't stand it anymore, she thought. I can't stand the way he gets away with everything. It's got to come to an end. If Rooney won't do it, then I will.

Instead of going back to class, Jeanie ducked out one of the side exits and headed for the parking lot.

Ed Rooney turned his car onto Portland Street. There were a thousand places a kid could go in Shermer when he decided to ditch, but an amazing number of them wound up at the Hot Dog Dump. So that would be the first place he'd look for Bueller.

The Hot Dog Dump was a low, wide building, painted brown on the outside with a big wooden sign of a hot dog in a bun on the roof. It was a popular lunch spot for secretaries and construction worker types, and as Rooney walked in the noise of the crowd and loud music from the jukebox bombarded his ears. Coming in from the bright sunlight, his eyes had difficulty adjusting to the dim lighting inside. It was hard to see faces clearly, but that did not stop him. He was a man on a mission.

Rooney pushed his way through the crowd, keeping his eyes moving. He saw a kid duck into the shadows near the phone booth. Could it be? Rooney grinned and followed. The kid saw him and ducked into the men's room.

Rooney pushed open the men's room door. The odor was powerfully foul. Even worse than the boy's room at school, if you could believe it. But at least the room was brightly lit and he could see.

A heavy construction worker with big pot belly was standing at a urinal, recycling a couple of lunch-time beers. Against the other wall were two closed toilet stalls. Rooney turned toward them. He knocked on the first. "This is Principal Rooney. Open up."

"Screw you, Jack," a heavy male voice replied.

Rooney assessed the voice. It sounded authentic. He moved to the second stall and knocked again. "This is Principal Rooney. Open up."

"Screw you, Jack." This voice was higher and trembling. Rooney smiled.

"You better open it, son," he said in his most menacing tone.

There was no reply.

"NOW!" Rooney shouted.

The door swung open and the kid tried to make a run for it, but Rooney grabbed him by the collar of his denim jacket and spun him around. "Okay, Buel—"

Rooney didn't finish the sentence. The kid wasn't Ferris. It was just some tenth-grader playing hooky.

"Uh, uh, Mr. Rooney," the kid gasped in terror, "I, uh, can explain..."

But Rooney had already turned and left the bathroom. He had bigger fish to fry.

Back in the Dump he continued to scan the tables. Over against the far wall a figure stood in the shadows at the video games. This time there was no mistake. Rooney crossed the room and sneaked up slowly on his prey. Oh, Bueller, my boy, I am going to give you the scare of your little cocky life, the principal thought. Just a few steps more and you're mine. All mine!

Rooney got right behind the video game player. "Gotcha!" he shouted, grabbing both arms so Bueller couldn't get away.

The player twisted around. It wasn't Bueller. It wasn't even a guy. It was a girl. And after she stopped looking so surprised, she looked vaguely familiar.

"Well, look who's here. Mr. Turdface Principal himself," the young woman said.

Rooney straightened up. "You can't talk to me like that, young lady."

"Oh, can't I?" the young woman said. "Maybe you forget, but I graduated last year and I can talk to you any way I want."

Rooney smiled. "Maybe so, but look at what you're doing with your life. Playing video games. That doesn't look to me like anything to be proud of."

"Oh really?" the woman said. "Well, it just so happens that I work for the company that leases and services these machines"—she pointed at a metal toolbox on the floor next to the video games—"and this year with overtime I'll pull down about forty grand while you run around chasing kids playing hooky."

"Forty grand?" Rooney scowled.

The girl smiled. "Yeah. One year out of high school. So go stuff yourself, Turdface." She picked up her toolbox and walked out.

One year out of high school? Rooney thought glumly. It took me twenty years to earn that kind of salary. Maybe I'm in the wrong business. Rooney shook his head sadly and told himself he needed a drink. There was a bar and lounge attached to the Hot Dog Dump, and he walked up to the bartender and ordered a beer. There was a television behind the bar and it was turned to the Cubs game.

"What's the score?" he asked, just as the bartender cracked open a beer and sprayed Rooney's face and chest with a fine stale foam.

"Zero to zero," replied the bartender absentmindedly, keeping one eye on the game.

Rooney didn't hear the reply because he was too busy licking the foam from his mustache and brushing the beads of beer from his lapels. "Who's winning?" he continued, trying to act as if nothing had happened.

The bartender turned away from the TV for the first time and gave Rooney a glare that clearly displayed his disgust over such a stupid question. "The Bears," he snarled, dismissing Rooney and turning his attention back to the game.

Rooney gulped down his beer and watched a couple of pitches. The batter fouled one into the upper bleachers. Rooney shrugged and turned away. He was going to find Ferris Bueller if it killed him.

18

"I GOT it!" Ferris shouted, jumping up in the stands at Wrigley Field. The pop ball loomed bigger and bigger as it spun back toward him. Around him other fans were reaching for the ball, but it seemed to be coming directly at Ferris. A split second later it slammed into his hands. Ferris held it up proudly. The crowd around him cheered. He wasn't certain where the TV cameras were, but he knew they'd be on him.

Down on the field, the umpire took out a new ball and handed it to the catcher. The crowd settled down again.

"Okay, show-off, you can sit now," Sloane said.

Ferris sat down and looked at the ball. On his right, Cameron was eating nacho chips covered with synthetic cheese. On his left, Sloane was concentrating on the next pitch.

Cameron popped another nacho in his mouth and looked at the ball in Ferris's hand. "See, if I had caught that ball," he said through a mouthful of nachos, "with my luck, Mr. Rooney would probably be watching the game and nail me."

"Cool out, you guys," Sloane said. "The runner on second is going to steal third."

115

Ferris and Cameron leaned forward to watch. Just as the pitcher started his windup, the runner on second sprang toward third. The throw from the catcher was high and the runner was safe.

Cameron sat back and stuffed another nacho into his mouth. "How did you know that was going to happen?" he asked Sloane.

"Simple," Sloane said. "I am a student of the game."

Ferris tossed the baseball in the air and caught it. "And I am a student of life," he said, handing her the ball and at the same time kissing her on the cheek. "This is for you. A token of my extreme esteem."

Sloane took the ball. She was glowing. "I can't believe you gave me your foul ball."

"For you, anything," Ferris said.

Sloane rolled her eyes.

"You don't believe me?" Ferris asked.

She shook her head.

"Name anything that is physically possible and I will do it for you," Ferris said.

Sloane thought for a moment. "What I want more than anything in the world is to get this ball autographed by Anton Rodriquez."

"Who's that?" Ferris asked.

"He's the Cubs' short relief man."

"Sounds like he cures indigestion," Cameron said, popping another nacho into his mouth.

Sloane smiled. "His job is to come in late in the game and snuff the other team."

"And where does this Anton Rodriquez dude usually hang out during the game?" Ferris asked.

"Over there," Sloane said, pointing to the dugout on the other side of the field.

Ferris snatched the ball out of her hand and stood up. "Then consider it done, my love."

"Sit down, Ferris," Cameron said. "You can't get a

ball autographed in the middle of a game. You'll have to wait until it's over. Then you can go stand around outside the players' exit."

Ferris shook his head. "It's the second inning and they're already losing fourteen to two. You really think we're gonna stick around to the end?" He turned and went down the aisle and out of the stands.

Cameron slumped back in his seat and watched the game.

"I love him," Sloane said dreamily.

Cameron munched on some more synthetic food. "It's hard not to. But this time he's not going to make it. It's impossible to get to the ballplayers during a game. Everyone knows that."

A bases-loaded triple with no outs made the score seventeen to two. Sloane called the ice cream vendor over and bought a cup. "It's difficult to stay interested in a game like this," she said across Ferris's empty seat to Cameron.

"If you ask me, it's difficult to get interested in games in general," Cameron said.

Sloane glanced at him. He really was a sweet guy. It made her feel bad that he was always so down. "Cameron, what you need is a girlfriend."

"I agree," Cameron said. "I just can't seem to be able to convince any girls of it."

Just then there was a murmur in the crowd. A lot of people were pointing across the field at the Cubs' bullpen. Cameron and Sloane both looked. At that very moment, someone was hanging upside down from the bleachers just above the bullpen. Two husky guys were holding his feet and lowering him. In one hand he held a baseball and in the other a pen. A couple of ballplayers in the bullpen came out and looked at him and the person handed the ball and pen to one of them. While the ballplayer signed the ball, the upside-down person chatted with the other players. Then he got the ball back and the two big guys lifted him back into the stands. The crowd cheered as the person shook the big guys' hands and then disappeared down one of the exits.

"He never ceases to amaze me," Cameron groaned.

Sloane smiled. "I know. Isn't he incredible?"

"I mean, I just can't believe that he did that," Cameron said. "First of all, no one else would even think of doing it. But not only does Ferris think of it, he goes right ahead and does it like it's the most natural thing in the world."

"For him it *is* natural," Sloane said. "He's the only person I've ever met who really believes that nothing is impossible. And it's almost like because he believes it, it comes true."

"I wish I could be like that," Cameron said with a sigh.

Sloane reached over and rubbed his head affectionately. "You're not so bad just the way you are, Cam."

Cameron grinned. "You mean it?"

"Yeah." She turned back to watch the ballgame. "Now watch the runner on first. There's going to be a pitch-out and he's going to be caught stealing."

But Cameron just sat back in his seat and smiled.

Suddenly two men appeared next to them in the stands as Ferris returned. One of them had short brown hair and a mustache and was wearing a yellow jacket, white shirt, brown tie, and brown pants. He had a stocky build and was carrying a black walkie-talkie. The other was a younger-looking guy wearing faded jeans and a green crewneck sweater. He was tall and thin and carried a thin green notebook. Ferris glanced at them and then handed the ball to

Sloane. "Here you are, my love. The ink is barely dry."

"That's cute, kid," said the man in the yellow jacket. "Now let's go."

"Go where?" Ferris asked.

"Out of the park," the man said.

"Why?" Ferris asked.

"Because you went into the bullpen and that's strictly off limits to unauthorized personnel," the man said.

"I never set foot in the bullpen," Ferris said.

"He's right," said the younger guy wearing the crewneck sweater.

"Who are you?" the man in the yellow jacket asked.

"My name's Tom Hunley and I'm a stringer for WLS," the guy said.

"The radio station?" Cameron asked.

Tom Hunley nodded.

"Well, this is none of your business," the man in the yellow jacket said. He turned to Ferris. "Now listen, kid, you can leave peacefully or I can have security throw you out. It's your choice."

"But I didn't set foot in the bullpen," Ferris said again.

"Well, you were in it," the man said. "It was on TV and everyone saw it."

"How do you define being in something?" Hunley asked. "I mean, if he didn't set foot in it."

The man in the yellow jacket looked annoyed. "Listen, buddy, don't get smart with me. He was in the bullpen. Everyone saw him. My orders are to remove anyone from this park who violates the rules. And being in the bullpen during a game is a definite violation of the rules."

Hunley took out his pad and started scribbling in it.

"Hey, what are you doing?" the man in the yellow jacket asked.

"I'm writing some notes," Hunley said. "Or are you going to tell me that's also against the rules?"

"Look, there's no reason to make a big deal out of this," the man in yellow said.

"I agree," Hunley said. "But I also think this is gonna make a pretty interesting story. What this kid did was not only within the rules, but it was a first for this ballpark and pretty ingenious, too. And not only that, but it looks like the only reason he did it was to get an autograph for his girlfriend. Imagine geting thrown out of Wrigley Field for being a romantic."

The man in yellow looked at Hunley and then at Ferris. Ferris smiled. The man looked disgusted. "Okay, just this time I'm gonna forget it. But don't do it again. Or else." He turned and left.

Ferris looked at Hunley. "Hey, thanks."

The guy grinned. "No sweat, kid, those park security guys are all puckered in the butt. Now listen, you can do me a little favor in return. You know who Lou Richardson is?"

"Sure," Sloane said. "He does the postgame shows on WLS. I listen to him all the time."

"Then you know that one of his features is having colorful fans on the radio after the game," Hunley said. "Well, he saw that little stunt your friend here pulled and he told me he wanted to get him on as soon as the game is over."

"Oh, wow," Cameron said.

Ferris grinned. "Sounds kind of cool."

"The station is downtown," Hunley said. "You can take a cab right after the game. They'll reimburse you for the fare."

"Great," Ferris said. "We'll leave right now."

Hunley looked surprised. "Don't you want to watch the end of the game?"

"Naw, three innings of baseball is all I can ever stand," Ferris said.

=== 19 ===

PRINCIPAL Rooney cruised slowly down Maple Street toward the Buellers' house. The large white colonial looked empty. There were no cars in the driveway. Still, it might have been a ruse. Bueller was probably in there right now, smoking pot with every truant this side of the lake.

Rooney parked his car on the street and walked slowly up the slate path to the house. It sounded pretty quiet. He stopped at the front door and listened. Not a sound. But then, Bueller probably had spies posted everywhere. He'd probably already been warned that the principal was coming.

Rooney pushed the doorbell and heard the chimes ring inside. A second later the intercom next to the doorbell crackled on.

"Who is it?" Ferris Bueller's voice asked.

So he's home after all, Rooney thought. He pressed the intercom. "This is Ed Rooney, Ferris. I'd like to have a word with you."

"I'm sorry I can't come to the door right now," Ferris's voice said. "I'm very ill and I'm afraid that in my weakened condition I could take a nasty spill down the stairs and subject myself to further school absences."

122

Rooney pressed the intercom again. "That's a lot of crap, Ferris. I want you to come down here immediately."

The intercom crackled. "You can reach my parents at their places of business. Thank you for stopping by. I appreciate your concern for my well-being. It will be remembered long after this illness has passed."

Rooney pressed the intercom again. "I'm not leaving until you come down and talk to me."

"Have a nice day," Ferris's voice said over the intercom.

"I'm not leaving, Ferris," Rooney said. He stood on the steps and waited. A couple of minutes passed. Rooney imagined Ferris inside with Sloane Petersen and who knew who else. They were probably laughing at the fact that the school principal was standing outside waiting for them to let him in. Or even worse ... they were just going ahead with whatever perversions they were up to, ignoring the fact that he was there. Rooney pressed the doorbell again. "Damn it, Ferris!" he shouted. "Open this door!"

The intercom cracked on. "Who is it?"

"Stop playing games with me, Ferris!" Rooney shouted back.

"I'm sorry I can't come to the door right now. I'm very ill and I'm afraid that in my weakened condition..."

It's a tape! Rooney suddenly realized, staring at the intercom.

"...I could take a nasty spill..."

The principal turned from the door. Now he had Bueller just where he wanted him. Pretending to be sick when he wasn't even home. Leaving this phony message on the intercom to make people think he was so ill he couldn't get out of bed was just the sort of thing Rooney expected of Bueller. He turned away from the door and got about halfway down the walk and then stopped. But wait, he thought. Maybe this is just a cover-up. If Bueller was in there doing something really devilish, then he'd want people to think he wasn't home. Rooney looked back at the house. Oh, you're a sneaky one, Bueller, but you can't outfox an old hand like me.

Rooney left the path and returned to the house. He squeezed through the bushes outside the living-room window and tried to peak in. The tape connected to the intercom was still playing: "... will be remembered long after this illness has passed." You'll remember me, Bueller, Rooney thought with a smile.

The principal inched his way around to the back of the house. Near the kitchen he noticed one of those little black rubber doors, the kind that let the family dog come and go as it pleased. The ground was muddy in the back and Rooney crouched down carefully, lifted the doggie door, and listened. Ah, what was that? He could hear something. It sounded muffled. He crouched down a little further. Was it a voice? He couldn't tell. The only way he'd know for sure was to get down on his hands and knees and stick his head inside the doggie door.

Rooney looked down at the mud and sighed. Damn, what he'd go through just to nail this kid. Well, it would be worth it, he was sure of that. He kneeled down in the mud, feeling the water seep instantly through the knees of his suit. Then he leaned forward and placed his elbows in the slime. There. Now if he could just get his head inside the doggie door ... The principal slithered forward in the slippery mud and managed to stick his head in the door. It smelled like a mangy old mutt down there, but at least he could see in the kitchen—the black and white tile on the floor, the bottom of the refrigerator, the cabinets under the sink, and the chair legs around the table. And that vague sound. Rooney tried to listen. It sounded like someone breathing. No, panting! No doubt it was Bueller engaged in some illicit sex act! And not only that, but the breathing was growing louder!

A second later a large black dog entered the kitchen, mouth open, panting. It turned and glanced at Rooney. For a brief moment the principal thought it smiled.

But the smile quickly turned into a snarl.

The problem with the Monte Carlo race, Igor thought as he shot down Dearborn Street, was that they had to go over the same course again and again. Being free to choose your own streets was much more fun. Suddenly he slammed on the brakes of the Ferrari.

"Whoa!" Sam White shouted. "What's happening?"

"Stuck," Igor grunted. Ahead of him, traffic was snarled.

"There's some kind of parade or something," Sam said.

Igor nodded and slammed the Ferrari into reverse. He whipped the nose around and headed back up the street. There was no way he was going to sit in traffic in a beautiful car like this.

20

FERRIS, Sloane, and Cameron were in a cab heading downtown.

"So what are you going to say?" Cameron asked.

Ferris put his arm around Sloane's shoulder and hugged her. "Well, first I'll answer his questions and then I'll take a few hours to discuss my personal view of life."

"What if he asks you about baseball?" Sloane asked.

"I'll just turn the mike over to you," Ferris said.

In the front of the cab, the radio was turned to the news. "In business news today," the announcer was saying, "trading volumes reached new highs at the Chicago Mercantile Exchange. Insiders reported that the burst of buying was kicked off when a mysterious financial expert shouted 'Buy!' from the visitors' gallery."

In the cab, Sloane and Cameron stared at Ferris, who grinned. Then he leaned forward.

"Hey, cabby, turn it to WLS, okay?"

The cabby nodded and quickly turned the channel. He looked like he was in his early thirties, with black curly hair and a dark complexion. "You say WLS?" he asked with a heavy foreign accent. "Is favorite radio station."

Ferris glanced at the name on the driver's hack license. Yuri Graboscowich. "Is that so, Yuri? So tell me, how long have you been in America?"

The driver looked at him in the rearview mirror and grinned. "One year."

"What's your overall impression?"

"Is good here," Yuri said.

"Better than Russia?" Cameron asked.

The driver nodded enthusiastically. "Much better than Russia."

Cameron looked at Sloane. "Obviously this man has never been inside an American high school."

"So what do you like most about America?" Ferris asked.

"Money, hot dogs, and *Penthouse* magazine," Yuri said with a big grin.

Ferris reached forward and patted the driver on the shoulder. "Well, Yuri, you obviously have your priorities in order. You sound like a man who's lived in this country his entire life."

"Thank you," the driver said. "Thank you, very much."

Ferris sat back and put his arm around Sloane's shoulders again. The cab had practically come to a halt in the traffic.

"Hey, what's the story with the traffic, Yuri?" Ferris asked.

"Is big parade today," Yuri said. "Is called German American Appreciation Day. How come is no Russian American Appreciation Day?"

"Your day will come, Yuri," Ferris said. "And in the meantime, we appreciate you."

Cameron was starting to chew on his thumbnail. "You know, Ferris. I really have to get the car home. I know you don't care, but it means my ass."

"You think I don't care?" Ferris asked.

"I *know* you don't care," Cameron said.

Ferris sniffed. "Aw, Cam, that hurts."

Sloane gave Ferris a nudge. "Come on, Cam's been a good sport today."

"You're right," Ferris said. He turned to Cameron to apologize, but the kid was staring out the window, his mouth agape.

"Cam, you're not going to barf those nachos, are you?" Sloane asked.

"Look," Cameron said weakly.

They turned and looked. Another cab was stuck in traffic right next to them and in the backseat Mr. Bueller was reading the paper. Cameron, Sloane, and Ferris were momentarily stunned. How could they possibly be running into Mr. Bueller everywhere today? Ferris's father started to lower the newspaper.

"Hit it!" Ferris shouted, throwing himself to the floor of the cab. Cameron landed next to him. Sloane stayed seated but shook her hair forward so that it obscured her face.

Ferris was lying on his back on the floor of the cab, staring up at the ceiling. Cameron was scrunched down on his face next to him.

"I can't believe this," Ferris whispered. "Twenty thousand cabs in this city and we wind up next to my father."

"What is problem?" Yuri asked from the front.

"It's nothing, Yuri. Just the KGB," Ferris said from the floor. Sloane's leg was next to his head. He poked it. "What's he doing?"

"He's looking at me and licking the glass and making obscene gestures with his hands," Sloane said.

"Ha, ha."

"I can't stay like this," Cameron whispered. "All the blood is rushing to my head."

"Roll onto your back," Ferris whispered.

A moment later they were both on their backs on the floor of the cab with their legs up on the seat.

"Is he still there?" Cameron whispered.

Sloane nodded. "You better stay down."

Several minutes passed. The cab had not moved an inch. Both Ferris and Cameron were starting to feel ill from lying on their backs with their feet up in the air.

"What's he doing now?" Ferris whispered.

Sloane looked out the window. "Well, let's see. He's taking out some rolling papers. Now he's got this little yellow envelope. He's tapping something green from the envelope into the paper. Now he's putting the envelope away and he's rolling up the paper. Oh, wow, he just lit up"—she looked down at Ferris—"I didn't know your father was a head."

"Very funny, Sloane," Ferris said. His shoulders were starting to hurt. "Listen, we're not getting anywhere in this cab anyway. What do you say we try it on foot?" He reached into his pocket and pulled out a ten and gave it to Sloane to give to Yuri.

"You get out here?" the cabby asked. "In middle of traffic jam?"

"Sure, why not?" Ferris said, pushing open the door on Cameron's side. The German American Appreciation Day parade rolled slowly down Dearborn Street, complete with floats, pretty girls in traditional Bavarian costume, and politicians in open cars. The marching bands played German folk music. Sloane and Cameron lost Ferris in the crowd.

"Where is he?" Sloane asked as they pushed their way through the throngs on the sidewalk.

"I don't know," Cameron said, "but at this rate we'll never make it to the radio station."

"Guten tag!"

It was Ferris's voice. They looked through the crowd but couldn't see him.

"No, guys. Over here!"

They turned around. Ferris was up on the German Beers float holding a stein of beer and tossing pretzels into the crowd. "Here you go." He tossed one to Sloane as he rode past.

Cameron started jogging alongside of the float. "Ferris, how—"

"My last name's Bueller, right?"

Cameron stopped and stared at him as the float rolled away down the street. "You're German American?"

"Someone in my family must've been," Ferris shouted. "Look. I'll meet you over on State Street in five minutes."

He shook people's hands as he went by, making small talk as if it were the most natural thing in the world. Ferris had a smile for everyone and the crowd responded to his good humor.

Sloane broke her pretzel in half and gave it to Cameron as they walked over to State Street.

"He's unbelievable," Cameron moaned.

"I know," Sloane said. "Isn't it wonderful?"

"Too bad you can't bottle it," Cameron said. "I know I'd become a Ferris Bueller addict if you could."

Sloane smiled slightly. "Listen, Cam, do you believe in reincarnation?"

Cameron shrugged. "I don't know. If I could become Ferris in my next life I might."

"Seriously," Sloane said. "Do you think you've ever lived before?"

"Oh, sure."

"Really?" Sloane asked, her eyes wide.

"Yeah, I was a tractor tire."

Sloane smirked. "I'm serious, Cam."

"Hey, so am I," Cameron said. "I was a Goodyear tractor tire, I rode on a John Deere manure spreader and at the age of three I ran over a pitchfork and was deflated for life."

"They say sometimes people are reincarnated as animals and vice versa," Sloane said. "I sometimes think in my past life I was a golden Lab."

"You must have been a pretty good dog to get reincarnated into you," Cameron said.

"Thanks, Cam," Sloane said. "What do you think Ferris was?"

"Easy," Cameron said. "He was Hannibal."

"From the A–Team?" Sloane asked.

"No. I mean the real Hannibal. The dude who rode the elephants over the Alps. Everybody thought he was crazy, but he did it."

"I think if he was anybody, he was Magellan. You know the guy who went around the world," Sloane said. "I could see him ignoring popular belief and taking off on some impossible mission."

Cameron nodded. "Yeah. For as long as I've known Ferris he's been the same way. Everything works out for him. There's nothing he can't handle. That's why he and I are friends. He can handle anything. Schools, parents, the future. You name it. On the other hand, I can't handle a thing. We're like Yin and Yang."

"You've really got a thing about the future, don't you," Sloane said.

Cameron nodded. "Yeah, like it's always there."

"I don't know. I guess it's different for a guy. Maybe the future is worse for you than it is for a woman."

"Why?" Cameron asked.

"Well, a woman can always bail out and have a baby and get some guy to support her."

"That sounds pretty grim," Cameron said.

"True, but it is an option. Having no options is worse."

Ahead was the corner of State Street. "I guess if I knew what I was gonna do, I'd feel better about this whole thing," Cameron said.

"There's college," said Sloane.

"Yeah, but to do what?"

"What are you interested in?"

"Nothing."

Sloane laughed. "Me, either."

"What do you think Ferris is gonna do?" Cameron asked.

Before Sloane could answer, they heard rock-and-roll playing loudly. They turned the corner and there on the pavement, the parade had stopped. People were dancing in the streets—cops, mothers with kids, teenagers, everyone. They were all caught up in the music, singing along and waving their hands in the air.

Ferris, of course, was in the middle of all the activity. Still on top of the float, he held a microphone in one hand, singing "Twist and Shout" at the top of his lungs. The crowd was going wild with enthusiasm—even the German band musicians had joined in the act.

Sloane looked at Cameron. "I think Ferris is going to do whatever he wants to."

They both laughed and Sloane poked Cameron in the ribs so that he turned to face her. She was twisting in place and Cameron couldn't help but follow. He didn't dance much, but he was having the time of his life improvising as he went along. He looked up at the float and gave Ferris a thumbs-up sign.

But Ferris was lost in his own little world.

As he sang, he grabbed one of the girls in Bavarian

costume and twirled her around. All the girls danced on the float, their black skirts flying up to reveal layers of white petticoats and lace. Ferris took turns dancing with each and never lost sight of the audience who was cheering him on, swaying in time with the beat. Ferris was ecstatic—all these people were caught up in *his* rhythm, and he with them. He was having the best high he could imagine as he belted out the next verse.

"Can you believe this?" Cameron asked Sloane as they pushed their way closer to Ferris.

"I've come to believe just about anything where Ferris Bueller is concerned," Sloane answered, her eyes staring at Ferris leading the local beauty queen in a finale performance.

"He's got all these people having a great time—they haven't a care in the world for five minutes and it's all because of Ferris. There aren't many guys who can break loose, believe in themselves and get others to do the same." She tucked her arm through Cameron's and gave him a little tug. "Even you're relaxed and enjoying yourself . . . No more thoughts about nuclear winter, right, Cam?"

"Yeah," Cameron said, and smiled. "Ferris does that to me."

21

THEY rode the elevator up to the studios of WLS and stepped out into a reception room. There was brown carpeting on the floor and leather couches and a row of windows with a pretty good view of the city. A large neon sign on the wall flashed WLS in big orange letters. Ferris, Sloane, and Cameron walked up to a wide wooden reception desk. A woman with curly black hair and wire-rimmed glasses sat behind the desk reading a *People* magazine.

"May I help you?" she asked.

"Yeah, I'm Ferris Bueller, the guy who got the ball autographed."

The woman gave him a funny look. "Congratulations, Ferris." She looked back down at her magazine.

"Uh, Lou Richardson wants to interview him," Cameron said.

The woman looked up again. "Because he got a baseball autographed?"

"Because of the way he got it autographed," Sloane said.

The woman scowled and flicked on an intercom. "Mary, there's a kid out here who says Lou wants to interview him. Something about getting a ball autographed...Oh, I see...All right, certainly." She hung up and pointed toward a pair of glass doors. "All right, you can go in."

The receptionist pushed a button under her desk that allowed Ferris to open the door. They went in and down a hallway, past promotional posters for the station and a lot of people sitting at desks talking on phones or typing. At the end of the hall a young guy wearing a blazer and tie was waiting for them.

"Hi, I'm Dave Goeffer," the guy said. "I'm working as an intern for Lou. You're the kid who got the autograph?"

"That's right," Ferris said.

"And who are your friends?"

"My bodyguard and makeup man," Ferris said.

Dave scowled for a second and then smiled. "Hey, it's cool. Follow me."

They went into a room filled with panels of electronic equipment and hundreds of dials and switches. "This is the control room," Dave said. He pointed to a woman with red hair who was sitting at a desk wearing a pair of earphones and quickly adjusting dials. Directly in front of her was a large plate-glass window.

"This is Muriel, our sound engineer," Dave said.

The woman looked up and nodded and then turned back to the dials. Dave pointed through the glass. "In there is Lou's studio."

They looked through the glass window and saw an obese man with a bald head and a goatee sitting at a table talking into a microphone. Muriel made some hand signs at the fat man, who was watching her as he talked. The man nodded back.

"Okay," Dave said. "He knows you're here. Now we just wait until he's ready for you to come in."

They stood behind Muriel and waited while Lou Richardson talked.

"What's an intern do?" Sloane asked.

"I run errands and junk," Dave said. "It's real slave work, but I want to get into radio after I graduate from college and it's good experience."

"You mean you're going to college right now?" Cameron asked.

"No, I took a semester off to do this," Dave said.

Cameron looked surprised. "They'll just let you take a semester off and go to work?"

"Sure," Dave said. "How can they stop you?"

Cameron shook his head and looked at Ferris and Sloane. "I never knew that. I thought it was another four straight years of school."

"If I had to do it all over again," Dave said. "I think I'd take a year off between high school and college. I mean, even with this semester off it's still almost seventeen straight years of school just to get a degree."

"An inhuman task," Ferris said.

Dave nodded. "Yeah, like parents always get real uptight and say that if you take a year off after high school then you'll never go to college, right? But what do they think you're gonna do, be an unskilled laborer all your life? All you have to do is take a year off and see the kind of crap jobs you get offered and you'll really want to go to college after that."

"Do you get paid?" Cameron asked.

Dave shook his head. "Are you kidding? The whole reason they have interns is because they know people are so desperate to get radio experience they'll work for nothing. Television is even worse. But that's why you have to do this stuff while you're still in school. You couldn't afford it otherwise."

Before they could discuss it more, Lou Richardson

made some hand signs and Muriel turned to Dave.

"He wants them to go in during the next commercial break," she said.

"Okay," Dave said.

The next commercial break came up pretty quickly and Dave led them into the room. The fat man slipped his headphones off and extended a meaty hand. "Which one of you is the one?" he asked in a deep gravelly voice.

Ferris immediately recognized the voice from the radio. Richardson was the most famous sports talk-show host in the Midwest.

"Me," Ferris said. "But I couldn't have done it without my trusty bodyguard and makeup man."

Lou Richardson didn't even blink. He just grinned. Dave told them where to sit at the table across from the talk-show host. They each had a mike and a pair of headphones in front of them.

"Don't put the headphones on until it's time for the phone-ins," the intern said. Then he turned to Richardson. "Need anything else?"

"Yeah, get me a pizza," the talk-show host said. He looked at Ferris and the others. "You like pizza?"

They all nodded.

Richardson looked back at Dave. "Get two pies. And some beer. And make it fast. I'm hungry."

Dave nodded and scooted out of the room.

"You kids ever been on radio before?" Richardson asked.

They shook their heads.

"Don't worry," the talk-show host said. "We'll have a great time."

Lou Richardson was true to his word. They had a great time, they ate pizza and drank beer, and Ferris got to talk about his personal philosophy of life.

"Now tell me, Ferris," Richardson said at one point.

"Why did you decide to be lowered into the dugout to get the ball autographed?"

"Well, I'll tell you, Lou," Ferris said while Sloane and Cameron munched on slices of pizza. "I may be a child of the eighties, but I'm an old-fashioned romantic at heart. And when my true love here said she wanted the ball autographed, I didn't stop for a second to think about it. I just followed my heart."

"Is he always like this?" Richardson asked Sloane.

"Always," Sloane said.

"Were you worried when those two guys lowered you headfirst into the bullpen?" Richardson asked.

"Worried about what?" Ferris asked.

"Well, worried that they might drop you twelve feet onto your head or worried that you might not be well received by the ballplayers?"

Ferris leaned forward. "I'll tell you, Lou. I know we're in an age of pessimism, but I for one still have faith in my fellow men."

"And women," Sloane added.

"It never even occurred to me that they might drop me," Ferris said.

Richardson nodded and wiped his lips with a napkin. The two pizzas had been divided evenly—one for the talk-show host and one for Ferris, Sloane, and Cameron. Richardson had it timed so every time Ferris talked he'd take one bite of pizza, chew it quickly, and swallow it just in time to ask the next question.

"So what do you think of the Cubs this year?" Richardson asked.

"To tell you the truth, Lou," Ferris said, "I don't follow baseball."

For the first time during the interview, Richardson looked surprised. "But you were at the game today."

"Oh, sure," Ferris said. "But it's not the game that

interests me. It's the experience, the gathering of humanity for a single cause, the partylike atmosphere—"

"And the nachos," Cameron said.

Ed Rooney had not climbed a tree since he was fourteen years old. And probably never in his life had he climbed one so fast. But the Buellers' killer dog had almost bitten his head off in that doggie door and Rooney had just had time to get up the tree before the dog got out and came after him. Now it sat under the tree looking up at him, smiling.

A florist's truck pulled up in front of the house and the driver got out. He looked young and had brown hair that fell over the collar of his white shirt. He was also wearing white pants and a white hat. He went to the back of the truck and took out a large floral arrangement. Then he started up the path to the house but paused when he noticed Rooney in the tree.

"Uh, how's the weather up there?" he asked.

Rooney smirked. "Very funny. Now how about doing me a favor and chasing this damn dog away so I could get down."

The delivery man squinted at him. "Say, aren't you Turdface Rooney, the principal?"

"I beg your pardon," Rooney said.

The guy smiled. "Oh, it's okay. I just remember you because you had me expelled in tenth grade for smoking in the boys' room."

"Smoking on school property is a serious offense," Rooney said.

"Oh, yeah," the guy said. "Anyway, I'm sort of glad you did it because I quit smoking pretty soon after that and haven't touched a cigarette since."

Rooney smiled. "Well, I'm happy to hear that, son. Now if you'd just do something about this dog, I really—"

"On the other hand," the guy said, "I always thought it was a real dippy thing of you to do. I mean, I could see getting a few detentions, or even being suspended, but who ever heard of expelling a kid for smoking?"

"As I recall, you were a repeat offender," Rooney said.

"Yeah, it was my second time, Turdface," the guy said. He walked over to the dog and petted it on the head. "If he comes down, bite him right on the ass for me, okay?"

The dog barked happily.

The driver took the flowers up to the front door and rang the bell. The intercom crackled. "Who is it?" Ferris Bueller's voice asked.

"Focus on Flowers," the driver said. "I have a delivery."

"I'm sorry but I can't come to the door right now. I'm very ill and I'm afraid—"

"It's a recording, asshole," Rooney said from the tree.

The guy turned and looked at him. "What's your problem?"

"He's one of my students," the principal said.

The driver looked at the card. "Little bugger's dying."

"What?"

"As I heard it from our mailman, he was supposedly born with only half a kidney," the guy said. "I don't know the details. But my boss had to send up to Milwaukee to get more orchids. He's very popular." He turned and knocked on the door.

"Save your knuckles," Rooney said. "Nobody's home."

"No?"

"No."

The delivery man walked back to the tree and looked up at the principal. "You gonna be around for a while?"

"I imagine so," Rooney said.

"You wanna keep an eye on these?" The delivery man handed him the flowers. "It really touches me that so many people are rallying behind this guy. I guess there's hope for the human race after all. Gotta run. Ciao!"

Rooney looked down incredulously at the floral arrangement in his hands. He flipped open the card that came with it: "All our best for a speedy recovery, the English Dept. Faculty and Staff."

Rooney groaned.

22

KATIE Bueller opened the door to the basement and flicked on a light. The air smelled
mildewy and the wooden stairs creaked
dangerously. With each step she wondered if the next
rung was going to give way and drop her onto the
floor. She glanced back at Dr. and Mrs. Hoffman, who
were following her on this final tour of the house.

"And as you may remember from our last visit,"
Mrs. Bueller said, pushing away some cobwebs, "the
basement has retained much of its original rustic fla-
vor."

She reached the floor without any of the steps giving way. The basement was very old. Parts of the
walls were nothing more than the original rock foun-
dation. There was a rusty three-speed bicycle and
some dusty storm windows. In the corner Katie noticed some rat droppings but didn't feel they were
worth pointing out.

"Looks like a dungeon," Dr. Hoffman said gruffly.

"I think it has great potential," said his wife.

Katie Bueller smiled. The Hoffmans had been fighting all morning. At the moment their darling son
Boyd was sitting out in the station wagon listening
to the radio. That was, if he hadn't already set fire
to the car.

"I think it would make a nice gathering room for Boyd and his friends," Mrs. Hoffman said.

"Maybe we could just chain him down here and lock the door," her husband said.

Katie smiled again. If I sell this house, she told herself, Ferris will be able to go to any college he chooses.

"Now Frank, you mustn't be so hard on Boyd," Mrs. Hoffman said. "It's just a stage he's going through."

Dr. Hoffman laughed. "When I was young, if a boy went through a *stage* like that he was thrown into military school until he straightened himself out. These days he gets an electric guitar, shaves his head, and has the right to cuss his elders."

"Times have changed, dear," Mrs. Hoffman said. She turned to Katie. "Didn't you say you had a son Boyd's age?"

Katie nodded.

"Well, isn't he a problem sometimes?"

"To tell you the truth, Mrs. Hoffman, Ferris is an angel," Katie said. "He's never caused us an ounce of trouble. On the other hand, Jeanie, my oldest daughter, is a real problem."

Mrs. Hoffman seemed pleased to hear that. "You see," she told her husband. "Every family has a problem child. We're not alone."

Dr. Hoffman nodded. "It's too bad we can't just anesthetize them from age twelve to twenty-two."

Mrs. Hoffman laughed nervously and looked at Katie. "Oh, he never means it when he says things like that."

"The hell I don't," Dr. Hoffman muttered.

Katie patted her hands together. "Well, is there any other part of the house you'd like to see?" she asked.

"Oh, I think we've seen enough," Mrs. Hoffman said. "We like this house very much, don't we Frank?"

Frank grunted. "For four hundred thousand I thought we'd get a little more charm and a little less rustic, but if this is what you want, so be it."

"Then I think it's time we went back to the office and discussed closing the deal, don't you?" Katie said, heading for the stairs.

She was relieved to see that the car had not burned to the ground while she and the Hoffmans were in the house. Boyd was slumped in the back, his feet up on the seat, playing with his lighter. He had dark sunglasses on. Katie and his parents got in the car. The radio was turned to that sports fanatic Lou Richardson on WLS, and Katie automatically turned it off as she got in. The car had a funny smell, sort of smoky and fragrant. Katie recognized the smell immediately because a few months ago she'd caught Kimberly smoking some pot in the attic.

Dr. Hoffman got in the car and turned to his son. "Did you burn something in here?"

Boyd shook his head.

"It does smell smoky," Mrs. Hoffman said.

"This Hari Krishna dude came by and tried to sell me some incense," Boyd said. "I told him to go roast his nuts on an open fire."

"That was very clever of you, Boyd," Katie said, starting the car.

"Hey, lady," Boyd said. "Did you say you had a son named Ferris?"

"That's not the way you address Mrs. Bueller, Boyd darling," his mother said.

"Okay, but does she?" Boyd asked.

"Yes, Boyd, I do," Katie said. "Why?"

"Well, he sounds like an outasight dude. Is he really climbing Mount Everest in September?"

"Not that I know of," Katie said.

"Aw, gee, you mean he was bullshitting?" Boyd said.

"Watch your mouth!" Dr. Hoffman shouted at him.

"How do you *watch* your mouth, numb nuts?" Boyd asked.

"Uh, what made you think he was climbing Mount Everest?" Katie asked.

"Really, Mrs. Bueller, I wouldn't pay any attention to him," Boyd's mother said. "He's at that stage where he thinks it's cute to bait adults."

"I don't think it's cute," Boyd said with a sneer. "I think it's fun. And anyway, it just so happens that this Ferris dude was on the radio just now and he said he had been selected by the president as the first high school student to lead the pledge of allegiance from the top of Mount Everest."

"That's quite amusing, Boyd," Katie said. "But actually, Ferris is home sick in bed at this very minute."

"Well, then some nut is running around the city claiming to be your son, lady."

Dr. Hoffman turned around, his face red. "Boyd, when we get home you're going to get the beating of your life."

Boyd picked his nose and flicked the goober at the ceiling of the car. "Oh, I'm scared, numb nuts, real scared."

Jeanie Bueller turned her car onto Maple Street. I can't believe I'm doing this, she thought as she parked in the driveway of her house. I am putting myself in a position where I could get expelled if I get caught, and it's all Ferris's fault. That little brat is making me do this for his own good.

Jeanie got out of the car and started up the front walk. Julian, the family dog, was sitting under the tree in front, happily chewing on a man's shoe. On the ground near him was a white sock and a piece of torn fabric that looked like it came from the leg of a man's suit.

"Hello, you disgusting smelly dog," Jeanie said.

Julian growled at her.

Jeanie pointed a finger at him. "After Ferris, my friend, you're next." Then she headed toward the house.

She quietly let herself in the front door. Surprise was an important element. It was now a proven biological fact that you could scare someone to death. It had to do with the body pumping an overdose of its own adrenaline into the heart during a moment of fright. Too much adrenaline could actually cause a heart attack.

You see, your honor, I was just coming home to make sure Ferris was okay. I didn't mean to frighten him so badly. And now I have to go through life knowing that I caused my brother's premature death. It's a burden I'm not sure I can bear.

If anyone is to blame for this tragic event, it is undoubtedly your brother, who should not have been cutting school in the first place. Case dismissed.

Oh, thank you, your honor.

Inside the house, Jeanie thought she heard a noise. She stood perfectly still. It seemed to have come from the kitchen. She smiled. Poor sick Ferris was probably fixing himself a little snack. Perfect. Maybe he was using a sharp knife. Maybe he'd be so surprised he'd accidentally cut his hand off.

I tried to stop the bleeding, your honor, but I was out of my head with panic. All I could do was just sit and watch that blood drain out of that beautiful young boy.

You poor, poor, girl. Case dismissed.

Jeanie crept slowly toward the kitchen. Ferris had just turned on the faucet in the kitchen sink. Jeanie counted to three and then leaped into the kitchen.

"Ah-ah!" she shouted.

"Huh?" said the strange-looking man standing by the sink.

Jeanie gasped. It wasn't Ferris. It was an intruder-burglar-rapist-molester wearing muddy, torn clothing! Jeanie used her forward momentum to spring into a karate stance and deliver a devastating side thrust to the face. The man went down with a thud and Jeanie ran upstairs and locked herself in her room.

She pressed her back to the door and felt her heart race in her chest. Thank God for tae-quan-do, she thought. But what if he comes up here after me? What if he has a gun? She quickly reached for the phone and dialed the police.

23

THE race was over. Igor knew he'd won when he covered the last six blocks in thirty-six seconds. The Ferrari shot down the street toward the parking garage.

"You goin' back?" Sam White asked.

Igor grunted.

"You got your yah-yahs out, huh?"

Igor smiled and nodded. "Da."

From the radio station they walked back toward the parking garage.

"Come to think of it," Cameron was saying, "I seriously can't believe you actually went on the radio. Do you know how many people must have heard you? You're nailed for sure now."

"Who would believe that I was on the radio?" Ferris said. "Who the hell am I? Besides, whoever would nail me doesn't listen to that station."

"My mother listens to that show," Cameron said.

"Your mother is in Decatur," Ferris replied.

At the parking garage office they paid the cashier. A second later the Ferrari flashed into the garage behind them and the two attendants jumped out.

Sloane turned around. "God, that was quick."

Cameron bent over and examined the car carefully.

"Looks okay to me, Cam," Ferris said.

Cameron straightened up. He looked relieved.

Ferris handed Igor another five-dollar bill. "We appreciate this. Good job."

Igor took the money and grinned. "You beautiful," he grunted.

"Thanks," Ferris said. He patted Cameron on the back. "Feel better?"

"Much," Cameron said.

Ferris held the door open and pulled the seat forward, but Cameron didn't appear really eager to climb in back. "Come on, Cam. This is probably the last time you'll have to ride back here. Keep that in mind."

Cameron shrugged and got in.

Ferris and Sloane got in front. A few moments later they were buzzing up Lake Shore Drive.

"So what's next?" Sloane asked.

"Nothing," Ferris said. "We return the car."

"We could go to my house," Sloane said. "My stepfather's on the road and my mother's not coming home until late. It's charity day."

"We have enough cash left for a quick flight to Peoria and back," Ferris said.

"Very funny," Cameron groaned.

Ferris glanced at the rearview mirror and changed lanes. His eyes caught the odometer. He blinked and looked again. Uh-oh. "Uh, Cameron, how many miles did you say this thing had on it when we left this morning?"

"Exactly one hundred and twenty-six miles and three tenths, why?"

"Oh, nothing," Ferris said, casually putting his thumb over the glass that covered the odometer. If I ever see that parking attendant again, he thought...

"Why?" Cameron asked.

"It's nothing, really, Cam."

"Then tell me why your thumb is covering the odometer all of a sudden," Cameron said. His voice was getting a panicky edge.

"Oh, I don't know," Ferris said. "I was just rubbing away a little piece of dust."

"I'm sure it's gone by now," Cameron said. "Take your thumb away from the odometer."

"Relax, Cam, it's no big deal."

"*Ferris, you know I can't stand suspense!*"

Ferris sighed. "Okay, Cam, I'll take my thumb away. Just don't scream."

The odometer read 432.7.

Cameron screamed. "*AAAAAAH!*"

Ferris had never heard a scream quite like it. It sounded like a water buffalo getting his nuts crushed. It was so loud and intense that he thought an ambulance was behind him.

"*AAAAAAAAAAAH!*" It was like an air-raid siren stuck in the on position.

"*AAAAAAAAAAH!*"

Ferris stared at Sloane with wide eyes.

"He sounds upset," he said.

"Yes, he does."

"*AAAAAAAAAAH!*" As abruptly as the scream had begun, it now stopped. In the car Cameron was frozen in a mindless, vacant stare. His arms were stiff at his sides, his eyes were bulging, and his mouth was wide open. You could see his tonsils.

"You okay?" Sloane asked anxiously.

He didn't answer.

"Hey, Cameron," Ferris said, worried. "It's okay. We'll fix it."

Cameron began hyperventilating. Sloane jumped

around in the seat, grabbed his arms, and began shaking him. "Cameron!" she shouted. "Cut it out! What's wrong? Ferris!"

Ferris pulled into the right lane and looked in the rearview mirror. "Cam, are you okay? It's no problem, really. Your old man won't know a thing. It's completely fixable."

It was a panicked and stressful moment and for once Sloane didn't believe him. "Shut up!" she yelled. "It is a problem. For him it's a problem. Nothing's a problem for you. But it's a problem for him! So just shut up!"

Ferris slowed the Ferrari down and pulled off to the side of the road. He knew Sloane was upset and he couldn't blame her for lashing out at him. But he would fix it. She'd see.

Ed Rooney opened his eyes. He was lying face down on a kitchen floor. There was blood in front of him. And mud. His face hurt, specifically his nose, which throbbed as if it was broken. Various other parts of his body were also wracked with pain. He tried to remember how he'd gotten there. He'd been in a tree. There'd been a dog. He'd jumped out of the tree and had tried to run for it. The dog had gotten him by the right leg. He'd lost his shoe, his sock, and part of his pants, but he'd managed to get away. He got into the house through a basement window. He'd gone upstairs to the kitchen and had started to wash the dirt off his hands and face when someone had burst in and bashed him in the nose. That was the last thing he remembered.

He slowly pushed himself up onto his hands and knees. Every part of his body hurt. In the distance he could hear someone shouting. It sounded like a young woman and it sounded like she was shouting into a phone. "This is not a phony phone call! There's an intruder, a male Caucasian, possibly armed, definitely weird, in my kitchen...What?...My name is Bueller...It's real nice that you hope my brother's feeling better, but right now I'm the one whose life is being threatened, you got that?...Listen, I'm very cute, I'm very alone, and I'm very protective of my body. I'd rather not have it violated or killed, okay? So I need help!"

Rooney managed to pull himself up into a standing position against the sink. His mind was in a fog. He wasn't certain where he was or why. He was just reaching for some paper towels to clean up the blood when the kitchen intercom blurted on.

"Uh, excuse me," the girl's voice said. "If whoever's in the house is still in the house, I'd like you to know that I have just called the police. If you have any brains you'll get your butt out of here real quick."

Ed Rooney reflexively stopped reaching for the paper towels and started toward the front door.

The intercom blurted on again. "I'd also like to add that I have my father's gun. And herpes."

Confused and half delirious with pain, Rooney stumbled toward the front door. As he reached it, the doorbell rang. He heard something click and then Ferris Bueller's voice said, "Who is it?"

"Wha?" The principal said.

"I'm sorry I can't come to the door right now. I'm very ill and I'm afraid..."

Rooney shook his head. It was like a nightmare. People coming out of nowhere and bashing you in the face, tapes going on and off. He reached for the door knob. All he wanted to do was get out. He pulled open the door.

Outside, there were three people on the front steps:

the flower man with another large bouquet of flowers, a balloon man with a huge bunch of balloons, and a woman dressed up as a nurse.

"Hi. I'm from the Nurse-O-Gram Message Service with a get-well message from your friends at school," the woman said. Then she sang:

> *"I heard that you were feeling ill.*
> *Headache, fever and a chill.*
> *I came to help restore your pluck.*
> *'Cause I'm the nurse who likes to ... dance."*

Principal Rooney launched himself off the front steps like a missile. He burst through the little crowd of well-wishers and started down the slate path to the street.

He had just reached the pavement when a tow truck with "Volbeck's Garage" stenciled on the side sped past. Hooked to the back was his car. Before he could even open his mouth to shout, it was fifty yards away.

Rooney started to walk. As he got to Primrose, a school bus turned the corner and pulled alongside him. The lady bus driver opened the door.

"Hey, Mr. Rooney!" she said cheerfully. "What're you doing?"

Rooney ignored her and kept walking. He wasn't sure what he was doing or where he was going. He wasn't even sure who he was. That blow to the face had really knocked his lights out.

The driver let the bus roll ahead and kept up with him.

"You get in a fight?" she asked.

Rooney still ignored her.

"Want a lift?" she asked.

Something clicked in Rooney's mind. A lift, he

thought. He stopped walking and looked up. The bus stopped next to him. He took a deep breath and climbed aboard.

He climbed in and looked down the rows of seats. Two dozen children stared back silently at him as if he had invaded their private territory. Strange, he thought. You'd think they didn't like me for some reason.

He sat down next to a skinny girl with braids and pigtails. She was the only one in the whole bus who grinned at him.

"I'll bet you never smelled a real school bus before," she said.

Rooney stared blankly at her. She held up a candy package.

"Gummi Bear?" she asked. "They've been in my pocket. They're real soft and warm."

Rooney closed his eyes and let his head tilt back. A moment later the bus lurched forward. He opened his eyes as if from a dream. On the ceiling of the bus, someone had scrawled in spray paint, "Save Ferris Bueller."

The principal sat up and looked around. What am I doing on this bus? he asked himself. A kid sitting across the aisle caught his eye.

"It's kind of like being in the belly of the beast, isn't it," the kid said.

Rooney blinked and stood up. "Stop this bus immediately!"

The bus driver hit the brakes and Rooney went flying forward.

24

FERRIS and Sloane stood on the shoulder of the roadway, watching the boats out on the lake. Ferris had his hands in his pockets. Sloane had one arm around his waist and was leaning into him. He was keeping an eye on Cameron, who was still frozen in the back of the Ferrari.

"You know what bums me out?" Ferris said.

"What?" Sloane asked.

"I knew that sooner or later this was gonna happen. Cam's always been a little keyed up. We're gonna graduate in a couple of months. And then we'll have the summer. He'll work and I'll work."

Sloane looked up. "You?"

"Well, I don't know. I mean, anything's possible. Look at that intern at the radio station. It could be an interesting experience."

Sloane rolled her eyes. "Go on."

"Anyway, Cam and I will probably see each other at night and on the weekends, right? And then next fall will roll around and he'll go to one school and I'll go to another. Or maybe he'll go to school and I'll go to Alaska. I don't know, but basically, that'll be it. I mean, as much as we like each other, the process of growing up will separate us. I know he doesn't accept that."

"I thought you never thought about the future," Sloane said.

"I usually don't," Ferris said. "Because the future usually isn't relevant. But this is relevant. Friendship is relevant. Because when it comes right down to it, the only thing we have in life is our friends."

"And lovers," Sloane said.

Ferris looked at her. "Do you really have to go back to Shermer next fall?"

Sloane shrugged. "I don't know, why?"

"Because I'd really like you to go with me," Ferris said.

"Where?"

"I don't know where, but wherever I go I'd like to have you along."

Sloane thought about it. "Well, you let me know where you're going and then I'll decide." She paused. "Now, listen, we better do something about Cam."

They went back to the Ferrari. Cameron was still in the back. He still looked as if he was frozen. His mouth was open, his eyes were wide, he wasn't moving. Sloane opened the door and reached in and stroked his hair.

"Cam, if you can hear me, I want you to know that I love you. Ferris loves you too. Think about that before you get too far away. Blink if you can understand me."

Cameron made no response. No blink, no nothing. He just sat there frozen with his mouth open.

Ferris got back into the Ferrari. "Get in, Sloane," he said. "This is worse than I thought."

Sloane jumped into the car and closed the door. Ferris put the car into gear and they lurched back onto the drive, leaving about two hundred feet of rubber.

"Where are we going?" Sloane asked. "A trauma center?"

Ferris shook his head as he floored the Ferrari. "I thought of that, but I think this calls for something bold, something wet, something wild."

They took Cameron to the Glencoe Beach Pier, but when that failed to shake him out of the trance, they headed for Sloane's house. Sloane lived in the nicest section of town, not far from Cameron's. Her house wasn't as modern or stark as Cameron's, but it did have a deck, a pool, and a built-in hot tub in the back. They took Cameron's clothes off and placed him in a chair next to the pool. Sloane went into the kitchen and came back with a couple of Pepsis, a bag of Oreos, and a blaster. She put the radio by the side of the hot tub and she and Ferris got in.

"You feeling any better?" Ferris called to Cameron.

He just stared into space, his mouth still open.

Sloane waved at him, but he didn't blink.

"I wish you'd wake up, Cam," she said. "The water's really nice."

There was still no reaction. Sloane and Ferris looked at each other and shrugged. Ferris found a good station on the radio and Sloane opened the bag of Oreos.

"Cameron," Ferris said. "Do you think this is because of the car? Or just a combination of everything shitty in your life just hitting you all at once?"

Cameron still did not respond. Ferris got out of the tub and took a can of Pepsi and opened it right under his friend's nose so the little bubbles fizzled up his nostrils.

"You just can't deal with it anymore?" Ferris asked. "The car took you into the ozone? Time for a reality check?"

Still no response. Ferris slid down in the water next to Sloane again.

"Cam?" Sloane said. "I could flip real easy too. There's nothing wrong with it. At one time or another, everybody goes to the zoo. Jimi Hendrix, Jim Morrison, James Honeyman-Smith, all the people you—"

Ferris cut her off. "They're dead," he whispered.

"Oh, right." Sloane winced and turned to Cameron again. "Sorry about that, Cam. But they were all musicians and you're not so it should be a lot easier for you to snap out of it."

Ferris groaned.

Sloane looked at him. "Convincing?"

"No."

Sloane turned back to Cameron. "Sorry, Cam."

"Maybe he was actually sick," Ferris said. "Maybe he wasn't just torturing himself."

Cameron was motionless. Then a little smile crept onto his lips. Sloane and Ferris leaned forward, curious. Splash! Suddenly Cameron keeled over forward and fell into the pool.

Ferris jumped out of the hot tub and dove into the pool. Below him Cameron was drifting down toward the bottom, a big smile on his face. Ferris swam down after him, kicking his legs and swimming madly. Cameron hit the bottom of the pool and just lay there smiling. Ferris reached down. His hand hit something soft and fleshy. Ferris grabbed it and pulled. A second later, they reached the surface. Ferris gasped for air.

Sloane was screaming. "Is he okay?"

"I don't know." Ferris grunted as he tried to pull Cameron out of the water. "Here, help me."

They dragged Cameron onto the wooden deck. For a second they couldn't tell if he was breathing. He was just lying there with his eyes closed.

Ferris leaned down and put his ear to Cameron's nose.

"What are you doing?" Sloane asked.

"Trying to tell if he's breathing."

"Do CPR, for God's sake," Sloane shouted at him.

Ferris looked down at Cameron's blue lips and wrinkled his nose. "On him?"

"Oh, you idiot." Sloane quickly pushed him aside and put her mouth over Cameron's. She started alternating breathing with cardiopulmonary thrusts. Meanwhile Ferris got on his hands and knees and put his lips just inches from Cameron's ear.

"Cameron, if you can hear me, don't deep-six on us, man. It won't look good on your attendance record. There's a lot of life ahead of you, man. I mean, just think, tomorrow you can go back to school... No, on second thought, don't think about that. I swear, if you come back to life I'll give you back all the money I ever borrowed from you. I'll even give back the Pink Floyd albums and the MTV satin jacket. Really, I swear I will."

Nothing seemed to be getting through. Ferris sat up and watched helplessly while Sloane worked feverishly on the CPR. Then he had an idea. He looked up at the sky. "Hey, you up there!" he shouted. "If this is some kind of punishment for ditching school, I promise I'll never do it again. At least, not again this year. Okay? Is that a deal?"

He looked back down at Sloane. She still had her mouth over Cameron's. Ferris looked back up at the sky. "Hey, I thought I just made a pretty good offer," he shouted. "What more could you want, huh? You want me to promise I'll never lie to anyone again? Not even dumb little white lies that don't hurt anyone? Okay, you got it."

He looked back down at Sloane. "Any sign of life?"

Sloane shook her head.

Ferris looked up at the sky again. "Okay, this is my final offer. I'll give you all of the above, plus I'll get a job and replace the bond I cashed in this morning. Now frankly, I think that's more than this dude is worth, but he's an old friend, okay? What do you say?"

Suddenly, Sloane sat back and gasped for breath.

"What happened?" Ferris asked.

"I think he'll be okay," Sloane said, wiping her mouth with the back of her hand.

Ferris looked at Cameron. His eyes were still closed, but there was a faint smile on his lips.

"You sure?" Ferris asked Sloane.

She nodded. He noticed she was grinning a little too.

"How do you know?" he asked.

"He slipped me the tongue," Sloane said.

Ferris gasped. He looked at Cameron. The kid now had a wide smile on his face. "Why you son-of-a—" Ferris remembered something and quickly turned and looked back up at the sky. "Wait a minute, I take it all back. The deal's off. Finished. Kaput!"

Cameron opened his eyes and looked up. "Too late," he said.

25

JEANIE Bueller sat on a hard wooden bench in the Shermer police station. Next to her sat a teenage head-banger wearing a T-shirt and suit pants. His hair was cropped short in places and long in others, and he wore silver studs and chains. He'd been staring at her since she'd gotten there and she wished he'd stop. She also noticed that he was sliding a little closer to her.

"Drugs?" he asked.

"No, thanks. I'm straight," Jeanie said.

"I meant, are you here for drugs?"

Jeanie just stared at him. Clearly she was not here for drugs. What planet did this creepo come from anyway? "Why are you here?"

"Drugs," the boy replied evenly.

It figures, Jeanie thought. "I don't know why I'm here."

"Then why don't you go home?"

"Why don't you put your thumb up your butt?" Jeanie asked.

The head-banger's expression did not change. "You want to talk about your problems?"

"With you?" Jeanie asked. "Are you serious?"

The kid nodded. "Yeah, I'm serious."

Jeanie moved a little further away. "Go blow your-self."

The head-banger seemed surprised. He crossed his legs and looked away.

Jeanie started to feel bad. Why was she being such a bitch to him? Well, as long as she was on a roll, she might as well continue her tirade. She looked at him. "You really want to know what's wrong?"

The kid shrugged and nodded.

"Well, to start off," Jeanie said, "I hate my brother. How's that?"

"That's cool," the kid said. "Did you shoot him or something?"

"No, not yet," Jeanie said.

The boy nodded as if he understood her feelings.

"I snuck out of school to go home to confirm that the little brat was ditching, and while I was there some guy broke into the house and tried to rape me. So I decked him and called the cops. Next thing I knew they dragged me down here for making phony phone calls."

"What do you care if your brother ditches school?"

"Why should he get to ditch school when every-body else has to go?" Jeanie asked.

"You could ditch too," the kid said.

"I'd get caught."

"I get it. So you're pissed at him because he ditches and doesn't get caught."

"Basically," she conceded. There was more to it than that, wasn't there, Jeanie asked herself.

"Then your problem is you."

"Excuse me?" Jeanie said. She must have heard him wrong.

"Excuse you," the kid replied. "You oughta spend a little more time dealing with yourself and a little less time worrying about what your brother does."

He noticed Jeanie's determined expression. "It's just an opinion," he added as an afterthought.

Who did this kid think he was? Why should *she* take advice from *him*? Jeanie was furious, partly because this punk was so cocky, partly because he was probably right. She didn't know what to make of him, so her first reaction was anger.

"There's somebody you should talk to..." the kid began to say.

Jeanie cut him off. "If you say Ferris Bueller, you lose a testicle."

The Ferrari was back where it belonged in its glass shrine, but not exactly the way it had been that morning. The rear end was jacked up and the engine was running. Ferris reached over the driver's door and held the clutch down with his left hand while he pushed the gear shift into reverse with his right. He slowly let the clutch out and the rear wheels started to spin backwards in the air. Cameron handed Ferris a brick and he laid it against the accelerator. The engine raced and the wheels started spinning faster.

Ferris backed away from the car and wiped his hands. "There, that ought to do it."

"How long do you think it'll take?" Cameron asked.

Ferris shrugged. "Awhile."

They sat down on the floor with Sloane and waited. The sun had already begun its downward arc toward the west and it was starting to get cool out. After absorbing the sun's rays all day, the tile floor in the garage still felt warm. Cameron lay down on his back and looked up at the ceiling.

"Feeling better, Cam?" Sloane asked.

"Yeah."

"What do you think happened to you?"

"I think I got so freaked that my brain forced itself

into a transcendental state," Cameron said. "Like that whole time I was just thinking things over. I was like, meditating."

"Bull," Ferris said. "You were torturing me for making you go out today."

"No. Not at all," Cameron said. "I'm glad you made me go. It was the best day of my life."

Sloane nodded. "It was a great day."

"Yeah, I'm gonna miss you guys," Cameron said.

Ferris was trying to rub a scuff out of his shoe with his fingernail. "Come on, Cam, admit that you weren't thinking all that time. Part of the time you were torturing me."

Cameron laughed and rolled onto his side. He propped himself up on his elbow. "Well, maybe part of the time. But I swear at first I was genuinely flipping. Then I sort of watched myself from the inside and I decided that it was ridiculous. Worrying about everything. Being afraid. Wishing I was dead. All that shit. I'm tired of it. That's why today was so great. I took a day off, I looked around and saw something other than doom and agony."

Sloane and Ferris both clapped. Cameron pushed himself up into a sitting position.

"I was so busy thinking about the future," he said, "that I never realized that it doesn't make any difference what happens later if the present is no good."

Sloane suddenly realized something and looked at him. "Did you watch me change into my bathing suit by the Jacuzzi?"

Cameron nodded and blushed a little.

Sloane stared at him, but a little smile creased her lips. "It's okay. I'm not embarrassed."

Cameron stood up. It seemed to Ferris that he had grown a few inches in the last few minutes. He

watched as his friend stuck his head into the Ferrari.
Cameron pulled his head out and waved for Ferris
to come. "The miles aren't coming off."

Ferris shrugged. "I thought it might be a problem.
It was a long shot. Tell you what. Let's crack open
the odometer and roll it back by hand."

Cameron shook his head. "That's something else I
figured out today, man. I gotta take a stand."

He walked around to the front of the car. "I've been
on this planet for seventeen years and I've never taken
a stand on anything. Never. I mean, I've been your
basic pussy. I put up with everything. My old man
pushes me around. He pushes my mother around. I
never say anything. I just take it and tell myself he's
a problem. But he's not the problem, I am. So that
part of my life is over. I'm gonna take a stand."

Sloane stood up.

"I'm gonna stand up against him," Cameron said,
looking down at the Ferrari. "And against my old
self, against my past, my present, and my future. I'm
not gonna sit on my ass as events that affect me un-
fold to determine the course of my life. I'm gonna
take a stand and I'm gonna defend it. Right or wrong,
I'm gonna defend it."

Cameron's face clouded over with anger and he
suddenly kicked the front of the car. Then he took a
deep breath and kicked it again.

The jack rocked forward. Cameron kicked the car
again and the jack almost gave in. The kid was going
berserk.

"I'm sick of it!" he screamed, his face turning red
with fury. He kicked it again and again. "I can't stand
him. I hate this goddamned car!"

His foot slammed into the Ferrari's bumper.

The jack tilted forward at a dangerous angle.

"You son-of-a-bitch!" Cameron screamed. He kicked it with all his strength. The jack tilted forward as far as it could without falling over.

Cameron leaned back to take another kick, but the rage had passed. He dropped his head and panted.

Ferris looked at Sloane and smiled, but she looked frightened. Cameron lifted his head and looked at them both.

"When my father comes home tonight, he's gonna see what I did and he's going to have to deal with me." He wiped some sweat off his brow. "I don't care. I really don't. I'm not gonna be afraid again. It's behind me."

Ferris smiled. Sloane looked at him and then at Cameron. A small smile appeared on her face.

Cameron grinned and shook his head. "To hell with him."

He lifted his leg and rested his foot on the bumper. Suddenly the jack gave out. The car toppled backwards onto the floor of the garage. The tires gave a high-pitched squeal and the Ferrari suddenly shot back in reverse. Cameron fell forward as the bumper flew out from under his foot. There was a huge crash as the Ferrari smashed through the glass and disappeared into the ravine below.

Ferris and Sloane walked over to the window, looked down at the car and then back at each other. They looked at Cameron who was trying to stand up, a look of dread in his eyes. He walked hesitantly toward the window, not wanting to see the havoc he had wreaked but unable to stand the suspense. Looking at his friends, he said, "What did I do... what did I do..."

"You killed the car." Ferris answered simply, still amazed his friend had actually acted out his rage.

Cameron looked down at the wrecked car, looked up, turned, and walked back into the center of the garage mumbling, "What am I going to do? What am I going to do?"

"Listen, it's my fault," Ferris said. "Let me take the heat for it. We'll wait here for your dad and I'll tell him I did it. He hates me anyway."

Cameron shook his head. "No. I'll take it. I want it. If I didn't want it, I wouldn't have let you take the car. I could have stopped you. It *is* possible to stop you, you know. I'll take it."

"It could be heavy," Ferris said seriously. "We're talking about one hundred and sixty-five thousand dollars worth of heat."

"I know," Cameron said. "It's okay."

Sloane leaned toward him and kissed him on the cheek. Ferris patted him proudly on the back.

"This boy has just made an appointment with destiny," he said.

"It's cool," Cameron said, looking calmer than he felt. "I'm loose." Cameron laughed, Ferris chuckled, and a nervous giggle escaped from Sloane as they all surveyed the damage. They knew Cameron was going to get it.

"She's never been in trouble before," Mrs. Bueller told the police officer as they stood in his glass-enclosed office. Katie could see her daughter sitting with the strange-looking boy outside the cubicle. "This is really a shock to me. First, I don't know why she wasn't at school. Second, I don't know why she'd call you with this story about a rapist," Katie continued, "and third, I don't know why she's putting her tongue down that awful punk's throat!" She stared out at her daughter kissing the head-banger. She wouldn't have figured the kid would be Jeanie's type—not that she was sure what her daughter's type *was*—but then perhaps there was a lot she didn't understand about her eldest daughter. Jeanie had never pulled anything like this in the past. "I just can't believe it," Katie said, shocked.

Jeanie could hear her mother talking with the police officer, but she paid them no attention. She didn't care what they were saying; she didn't care about Ferris and his shenanigans or about getting even with her brother. All she cared about was the blissful moment she was sharing with this kid she had just met. She prolonged every minute of the kiss, instinctively pulling his head to hers and responding to his passion.

"For whatever reason she did it," the police officer said, "I think she's had a good scare."

"I hope so," Katie Bueller said firmly. "And I really appreciate your calling me. I can assure you that her father and I will have a long talk with her." She gathered up her purse and was about to leave the office when the policeman caught her arm.

A tender look of sympathy was in his eyes as he said, "And by the way, I hope your son is feeling better."

Katie gave him a curious look.

"Tell him all the guys at the station are pulling for him," he added.

Katie just nodded and turned around. How did *everyone* know Ferris was out sick today?

A second later, Jeanie heard the door open. She broke the embrace with the head-banger of her dreams.

"If you can keep this to yourself," Jeanie whispered to him, "I think we can probably get it on pretty good."

"For sure," the kid replied, trying to adjust his

pants so no one would notice how excited he'd gotten from Jeanie's kiss.

Mrs. Bueller came out of the office looking sore, but Jeanie only smiled dreamily at her. "Hi, Mom."

"Don't 'Hi, Mom' me, young lady," Katie snapped. "Get your stuff."

Jeanie stood up and turned to say good-bye to her head-banger.

"Can I see you again?" he whispered.

"Yes," Jeanie whispered back as she reached down for her purse. "I can sneak out tonight after everyone's asleep. Where should we meet?"

"I don't know," the head-banger said. "I may be in jail."

Jeanie giggled.

"Hey what's your name?" the guy asked.

"Jean. What's yours?"

"Garth Volbeck."

She gave him a sweet smile and then left with her mother. They walked out to the station wagon together, and Jeanie offered to drive home. Katie went around to the passenger side, got in, and opened her briefcase. As the car pulled away she ruffled through some papers, mumbling something about closing a deal. Jeanie stared straight ahead, a smile curving her lips as she thought about Garth and their spontaneous interlude.

Ferris and Sloane left Cameron's house and headed down the road.

"I had a great time today," Sloane said as they walked.

"Yeah." Ferris agreed. "It was pretty cool."

"You think Cameron's gonna be all right?"

"For the first time in his life," Ferris said. "He had to do it. It's okay."

"You knew what you were doing when you woke up this morning, didn't you?" Sloane asked.

Ferris just smiled.

"You think he'll really stand up to his father?"

"To misquote a great man," Ferris said looking at her, "'he has nothing to fear but fear itself.'"

"Franklin Delano Roosevelt," Sloane said.

"The guy knew what he was talking about," Ferris said.

"Somehow I just have this picture of Mr. Frye coming home and beating the crap out of him," Sloane said.

"A great man said, 'You can break a man, but you can never break his spirit,'" Ferris said.

"I'll have to look that one up," Sloane said.

When they reached her house the sun was setting. Sloane and Ferris stopped at the foot of the driveway.

"Maybe we could ditch again next week," Sloane said.

Ferris shook his head. "Today was it for me."

Sloane looked at him. "You mean, because of that promise you made?"

Ferris shrugged. "No. But there were too many near misses today. I had a great time, but I don't want to push it. Like, you gotta know when to quit. Besides, school's over in three months and then we'll have the whole summer. In the meantime there's a weekend every five days. We'll just have to make do."

Sloane gave him a skeptical look.

"Hey," Ferris said. "If you ditch too much, it gets to be the same old thing after a while, right? Just like school. Besides, we have all next year."

"What do you mean?" Sloane asked.

Ferris took her in his arms. "I mean next year you'll be a senior at Shermer and I'll be off at college somewhere and we'll have to do a whole load of ditching if we expect to keep this thing going."

Sloane hugged him. "Ferris, I love you."

Ferris smiled. "Yeah."

She looked at her watch. "Guess I better go in."

"What time is it?" Ferris asked casually.

"Almost six."

Ferris suddenly felt the blood drain from his face. "Shit!" he gasped. "I gotta go." He started to run, then looked back over his shoulder. "I'll call you tonight."

"I love you," Sloane shouted back behind him. She turned to go into her house. He's gonna marry me, she thought. I know it.

Ferris was halfway down the block, hoofing it as fast as his legs could carry him. He cut through backyards, jumped over fences, ran through a family's outdoor barbeque, and outran a yapping French poodle. He got to the intersection of Maple Street and Primrose just as Jeanie and Katie turned the corner in the station wagon. He was running so quickly he couldn't stop, and as Jeanie slammed on the brakes, he rolled on top of the hood and over the side of the car. Katie's papers had gone flying and her briefcase slipped onto the floor. In the confusion she hadn't noticed the kid. But Jeanie did. She locked her eyes with Ferris's when he stood for a moment, staring at her behind the wheel. Within five seconds he had been off and running.

Jeanie's eyes had opened wide, her hands clenched the steering wheel, and she floored the car. Katie lurched forward once again, her briefcase slamming into the dashboard.

She turned to look at Jeanie, who had a crazed look on her face as she sped along the side streets to their house. Katie didn't know what had come over her daughter and braced herself for the frenzied ride home.

Ferris ran faster. He had to get home before Jeanie did. Otherwise he was dead meat. Kids on dirt bikes followed him, amazed at Ferris's speed, determined to stay with him. Just as he reached the yard, he saw his mother's car come barreling down the street. His house was in view now and he could see his father's Audi coming down Maple from the opposite direction. Ferris slowed to a jog. There was no way he could beat them into the house.

Then a small miracle occurred. Both of his parents' cars got to the house at the same exact moment. They stopped on the street, each waiting for the other to turn into the driveway first. Ferris started to run again. He had a chance. It wasn't much of a chance, but it was worth a try.

He cut behind the next-door neighbors' house and ran through their backyard to his own house. He grabbed the back door and twisted the doorknob. It wouldn't open; the damn thing was locked! Ferris dropped to his knees and quickly lifted the rubber mat at the doorstep. But there was no key, only the outline in the dirt of where the key had once been.

Just then a pair of chewed-up dress shoes stepped into his field of vision. Ferris froze and slowly looked up into the swollen and bruised face of Ed Rooney. In his hand, the principal held the back-door key. He was smiling fiendishly.

"Looking for this?" Rooney asked.

"Yes," Ferris said weakly. He was done for, finished, kaput. The game was over. He'd finally been nailed.

Rooney gloated over his victory. "I got you, Ferris.

This time I finally got you. I've been waiting for this. I've been dreaming about this. And, goddamn, you little bastard, I got you right where I want you."

Ferris nodded. Life was a game, and if you were going to enjoy the wins you were also going to have to accept a few losses.

Jeanie beat her parents into the house. Intuition told her to head for the back door. She pushed back the curtain and saw Rooney and Ferris outside. I can't believe it, she thought. He finally got caught.

"How does another year of high school sit with you?" Rooney asked, savoring the moment. He had waited too long.

The idea made Ferris cringe.

Suddenly the back door burst open and Jeanie rushed out. "Oh, Ferris!" She hugged him. "Thank God you're all right! We were worried sick!"

"Wha?" Rooney gasped. He looked from Jeanie to Ferris, not quite certain he was seeing and hearing properly.

It took Ferris a second to catch on. Then he grinned. Horray for the home team!

Meanwhile, Jeanie looked at the principal. "Thank you for bringing him home, Mr. Rooney." Then she turned to Ferris. "You better get up to bed right now."

Ferris was grinning from ear to ear. Jeanie winked at him. As he started into the house, he heard his sister tell Rooney, "Can you imagine someone as sick as Ferris trying to walk home from the hospital?"

Rooney stared at Jeanie. Her eyes twinkled with excitement, her lips quivering as she tried not to laugh at Rooney. He looked so defeated, so tired, so bewildered. Will I ever win? He wondered as he slumped away. I was within inches of nailing that brat once and for all, he thought. And now...His entire body quivered as the anger rose from the soles of his muddy wingtips to the top of his scalp, where his hair blew in all directions, exposing the beginnings of a shiny pink bald spot.

And all because of Jeanie, he muttered. Wasn't she always out to make Ferris look bad, anyway? Why now, of all times, did she rush to his side. Why now? Rooney cursed himself for ever taking a job that involved kids. Why hadn't he chosen a respectable profession—like repairing video games?

He glanced back and saw Jeanie strike a karate pose in the kitchen. She looked him straight in the eye and in that moment he knew she had been the one who attacked him earlier. He was sure he'd never win. He left.

Ferris ran upstairs to his room and flicked on the computer. Downstairs the garage door was going up. Ferris punched out the commands to disengage the doorbell from the tape recorder. Now he could hear voices downstairs in the kitchen. He jumped away from the computer and pulled the mannequin out of his bed. Then he spread his schoolbooks out on the floor. He was just about to start undressing when he heard footsteps coming up the stairs. Shit! He threw himself in the bed with his clothes on and pulled the blanket up.

Ricky and Kimberly were the first ones up the steps.

"Ferris!" they shouted as they came into his room.

"Oh, hi," he said, weakly.

Kimberly reached over and felt his forehead, then quickly pulled her hand away. "Oh, gross, you're all wet."

It was sweat from running all the way from Sloane's house. "It's just from the fever," he said.

"Hey, Ferris," Ricky said. "Does my head look like it's getting any bigger?"

Ferris looked at his little brother and then at his little sister. "No, but Kim's sure is."

Kimberly screamed and grabbed her head. She turned to run out of the room just as Mrs. Bueller came in.

"Stop screaming, Kim," her mother said. "How is your brother?"

"His head's all wet," Kim cried, "and mine's growing."

Katie Bueller gave her a pat on the rear. "Okay, go downstairs. You too, Ricky." Then she went to Ferris's bedside and touched his forehead.

"It's just from the fever, Mom," Ferris said weakly. "But it's broken. I've beaten it."

Now Tom Bueller joined them. "How is he?"

"I'm better, Dad, really," Ferris said, trying to sit up. The blanket slid down. He was concentrating so hard on his act that he forgot he had his clothes on.

His father scowled. "You're dressed."

Ferris looked down at himself. "Oh, uh, I had the chills. Couldn't keep warm."

Mrs. Bueller nodded. "First the chills, then the sweats. You must have some bug."

"But I'm a hundred and fifty percent better," Ferris said. "Please don't make me stay home again. I want to go to school. I'm graduating in June and I—"

Tom gently pushed Ferris back into the bed and tucked the blanket up around his chin. "Ferris, you're sick. There's no point in pushing yourself and making it worse."

Ferris nodded. "Maybe you're right, Dad."

"I know I'm right, pal," his father said.

His mother leaned over and kissed him on the forehead. "How did you get so sweet?"

Ferris smiled at her. "Years of practice, Mom."

His father bent down and patted him on the shoulder. Then his parents turned and left the room. Ferris rolled over on his back and put his hands behind his head. "I said it before and I'll say it again, Life moves pretty fast. If you don't stop and look around every once in a while, you could miss it."